Dear Santha,
    Best wishes for a
very happy birthday,
Aniappappan,
Annie kochamma,
            Oct. 30, 1993

KIPLING STORIES AND POEMS

KIPLING

STORIES AND POEMS

Illustrated by
Kurt Wiese, J. M. Gleeson,
Charles Livingston Bull
and the Author

BARNES
&NOBLE
BOOKS
NEW YORK

This Edition
of This Book Is Dedicated
to the Memory of the Author
Who Wrote For All Ages
and For All Time.

This edition published by Barnes & Noble, Inc.,
by arrangement with Doubleday & Company, Inc. a division of
Bantam, Doubleday, Dell Publishing Group Inc.

1993 Barnes & Noble Books

ISBN 1-56619-072-X

Printed and bound in the United States of America

M 9 8 7 6 5 4 3 2 1

CONTENTS

From *Just So Stories*

CONTENTS

CONTENTS

ILLUSTRATIONS

BY KURT WIESE

ILLUSTRATIONS

BY RUDYARD KIPLING

ILLUSTRATIONS

Now these are the Laws of the Jungle,
And many and mighty are they;
But the head and the hoof of the Law
And the haunch and the hump is—
                              "OBEY!"

I

THE ELEPHANT'S CHILD

From *Just So Stories*

IN THE High and Far-Off Times the Elephant, O Best Beloved, had no trunk. He had only a blackish, bulgy nose, as big as a boot, that he could wriggle about from side to side; but he could n't pick up things with it. But there was one Elephant—a new Elephant—an Elephant's Child—who was full of 'satiable curtiosity, and that means he asked ever so many questions. *And* he lived in Africa, and he filled all Africa with his 'satiable curtiosities. He asked his tall aunt, the Ostrich, why her tail-feathers grew just so, and his tall aunt the Ostrich spanked him with her hard, hard claw. He asked his tall uncle, the Giraffe, what made his skin spotty, and his tall uncle, the Giraffe, spanked him with his hard, hard hoof. And still he was full of 'satiable curtiosity! He asked his broad aunt, the Hippopotamus, why her eyes were red, and his broad aunt, the Hippopotamus, spanked him with her broad, broad hoof; and he asked his hairy uncle, the Baboon, why melons tasted just so, and his hairy uncle, the Baboon, spanked him with his hairy, hairy paw. And *still* he was full of 'satiable curtiosity! He asked questions about everything that he saw, or heard, or felt, or smelt, or touched, and all his uncles and his aunts spanked him. And still he was full of 'satiable curtiosity!

"The Ostrich spanked him with her hard, hard claw."

One fine morning in the middle of the Precession of the Equinoxes, this 'satiable Elephant's Child asked a new fine question that he had never asked before. He asked, "What does the Crocodile have for dinner?" Then everybody said, "Hush!" in a loud and dretful tone, and they spanked him immediately and directly, without stopping, for a long time.

By and by, when that was finished, he came upon Kolokolo Bird sitting in the middle of a wait-a-bit thorn-bush, and he said, "My father has spanked me, and my mother has spanked me; all my aunts and uncles have spanked me for my 'satiable curtiosity; and *still* I want to know what the Crocodile has for dinner!"

Then Kolokolo Bird said, with a mournful cry, "Go to the banks of the great gray-green, greasy Limpopo River, all set about with fever-trees, and find out."

That very next morning, when there was nothing left of the Equinoxes, because the Precession had preceded according to precedent, this 'satiable Elephant's Child took a hundred pounds of bananas (the little short red kind), and a hundred pounds of sugar-cane (the long purple kind), and seventeen melons (the greeny-crackly kind), and said to all his dear families, "Good-bye. I am going to the great gray-green, greasy Limpopo River, all set about with fever-trees, to find out what the Crocodile has for dinner." And they all spanked him once more for luck, though he asked them most politely to stop.

"The Giraffe spanked him with his hard, hard hoof."

Then he went away, a little warm, but not at all astonished, eating melons, and throwing the rind about, because he could not pick it up.

He went from Graham's Town to Kimberley, and from Kimberley to Khama's Country, and from Khama's Country he went east by north, eating melons all the time, till at last he came to the banks of the great gray-green, greasy Limpopo River, all set about with fever-trees, precisely as Kolokolo Bird had said.

Now you must know and understand, O Best Beloved, that till that very week, and day, and hour, and minute, this 'satiable Elephant's Child had never seen a Crocodile, and did not know what one was like. It was all his 'satiable curtiosity.

The first thing that he found was a Bi-Coloured-Python-Rock-Snake curled round a rock.

" 'Scuse me," said the Elephant's Child most politely, "but have you seen such a thing as a Crocodile in these promiscuous parts?"

"*Have* I seen a Crocodile?" said the Bi-Coloured-Python-Rock-Snake, in a voice of dretful scorn. "What will you ask me next?"

"The Baboon spanked him with his hairy, hairy paw"

"The Hippopotamus spanked him with her broad, broad hoof"

" 'Scuse me," said the Elephant's Child, "but could you kindly tell me what he has for dinner?"

Then the Bi-Coloured-Python-Rock-Snake uncoiled himself very quickly from the rock, and spanked the Elephant's Child with his scalesome, flailsome tail.

"That is odd," said the Elephant's Child, "because my father and my mother, and my uncle and my aunt, not to mention my other aunt, the Hippopotamus, and my other uncle, the Baboon, have all spanked me for my 'satiable curtiosity—and I suppose this is the same thing."

So he said good-bye very politely to the Bi-Coloured-Python-Rock-Snake, and helped to coil him up on the rock again, and went on, a little warm, but not at all astonished, eating melons, and throwing the rind about, because he could not pick it up, till he trod on what he thought was a log of wood at the very edge of the great gray-green, greasy Limpopo River, all set about with fever-trees.

But it was really the Crocodile, O Best Beloved, and the Crocodile winked one eye—like this!

" 'Scuse me," said the Elephant's Child most politely, "but do you happen to have seen a Crocodile in these promiscuous parts?"

Then the Crocodile winked the other eye, and lifted half his tail out of the mud; and the Elephant's Child stepped back most politely, because he did not wish to be spanked again.

"Come hither, Little One," said the Crocodile. "Why do you ask such things?"

" 'Scuse me," said the Elephant's Child most politely, "but my father has spanked me, my mother has spanked me, not to mention my tall aunt, the Ostrich, and my tall uncle, the Giraffe, who can kick ever so hard, as well as my broad aunt, the Hippopotamus, and my hairy uncle, the Baboon, *and* including the Bi-Coloured-Python-Rock-Snake, with the scalesome, flailsome tail, just up the bank, who spanks harder than any of them; and *so*, if it 's quite all the same to you, I don't want to be spanked any more."

"Come hither, Little One," said the Crocodile, "for I am the Crocodile," and he wept crocodile-tears to show it was quite true.

Then the Elephant's Child grew all breathless, and panted, and kneeled down on the bank and said, "You are the very person I have been looking for all these long days. Will you please tell me what you have for dinner?"

"Come hither, Little One," said the Crocodile, "and I 'll whisper."

Then the Elephant's Child put his head down close to the Crocodile's musky, tusky mouth, and the Crocodile caught him by his little nose, which up to that very week, day, hour, and minute, had been no bigger than a boot, though much more useful.

"I think," said the Crocodile—and he said it between his teeth, like this—"I think to-day I will begin with Elephant's Child!"

At this, O Best Beloved, the Elephant's Child was much annoyed, and he said, speaking through his nose, like this, "Led go! You are hurtig be!"

Then the Bi-Coloured-Python-Rock-Snake scuffled down from the bank and said, "My young friend, if you do not now, immediately and instantly, pull as hard as ever you can, it is my opinion that your acquaintance in the large-pattern leather ulster" (and by this he meant the Crocodile) "will jerk you into yonder limpid stream before you can say Jack Robinson."

This is the way Bi-Coloured-Python-Rock-Snakes always talk.

Then the Elephant's Child sat back on his little haunches, and pulled, and pulled, and pulled, and his nose began to stretch. And the Crocodile floundered into the water, making it all creamy with great sweeps of his tail, and *he* pulled, and pulled, and pulled.

And the Elephant's Child's nose kept on stretching; and the Elephant's Child spread all his little four legs and pulled, and pulled, and pulled, and his nose kept on stretching; and the Crocodile threshed his tail like an oar, and *he* pulled, and pulled, and pulled, and at each pull the Elephant's Child's nose grew longer and longer—and it hurt him hijjus!

Then the Elephant's Child felt his legs slipping, and he said through his nose, which was now nearly five feet long, "This is too butch for be!"

Then the Bi-Coloured-Python-Rock-Snake came down from the bank, and knotted himself in a double-clove-hitch, round the Elephant's Child's hind legs, and said, "Rash and

inexperienced traveller, we will now seriously devote ourselves to a little high tension, because if we do not, it is my
impression that yonder self-propelling man-of-war with the
armour-plated upper deck" (and by this, O Best Beloved, he
meant the Crocodile), "will permanently vitiate your future
career."

That is the way all Bi-Coloured-Python-Rock-Snakes
always talk.

So he pulled, and the Elephant's Child pulled, and the
Crocodile pulled; but the Elephant's Child and the Bi-
Coloured-Python-Rock-Snake pulled hardest; and at last
the Crocodile let go of the Elephant's Child's nose with a
plop that you could hear all up and down the Limpopo.

Then the Elephant's Child sat down most hard and sudden;
but first he was careful to say "Thank you" to the Bi-
Coloured-Python-Rock-Snake; and next he was kind to his
poor pulled nose, and wrapped it all up in cool banana leaves,
and hung it in the great gray-green, greasy Limpopo to cool.

"What are you doing that for?" said the Bi-Coloured-
Python-Rock-Snake.

" 'Scuse me," said the Elephant's Child, "but my nose is
badly out of shape, and I am waiting for it to shrink."

"Then you will have to wait a long time," said the Bi-
Coloured-Python-Rock-Snake. "Some people do not know
what is good for them."

The Elephant's Child sat there for three days waiting for
his nose to shrink. But it never grew any shorter, and, besides,
it made him squint. For, O Best Beloved, you will see and
understand that the Crocodile had pulled it out into a really
truly trunk same as all Elephants have to-day.

At the end of the third day a fly came and stung him on
the shoulder, and before he knew what he was doing he lifted
up his trunk and hit that fly dead with the end of it.

This is the Elephant's Child having his nose pulled by the Crocodile. He is much surprised and astonished and hurt, and he is talking through his nose and saying, "Led go! You are hurtig be!" He is pulling very hard, and so is the Crocodile; but the Bi-Coloured-Python-Rock-Snake is hurrying through the water to help the Elephant's Child. All that black stuff is the banks of the great gray-green, greasy Limpopo River (but I am not allowed to paint these pictures), and the bottly-tree with the twisty roots and the eight leaves is one of the fever-trees that grow there.

Underneath the truly picture are shadows of African animals walking into an African ark. There are two lions, two ostriches, two oxen, two camels, two sheep, and two other things that look like rats, but I think they are rock-rabbits. They don't mean anything. I put them in because I thought they looked pretty. They would look very fine if I were allowed to paint them.

27

" 'Vantage number one!" said the Bi-Coloured-Python-Rock-Snake. "You could n't have done that with a mere-smear nose. Try and eat a little, now."

Before he thought what he was doing the Elephant's Child put out his trunk and plucked a large bundle of grass, dusted it clean against his fore-legs, and stuffed it into his own mouth.

" 'Vantage number two!" said the Bi-Coloured-Python-Rock-Snake. "You could n't have done that with a mere-smear nose. Don't you think the sun is very hot here?"

"It is," said the Elephant's Child, and before he thought what he was doing he schlooped up a schloop of mud from the banks of the great gray-green, greasy Limpopo, and slapped it on his head, where it made a cool schloopy-sloshy mud-cap all trickly behind his ears.

" 'Vantage number three!" said the Bi-Coloured-Python-Rock-Snake. "You could n't have done that with a mere-smear nose. Now how do you feel about being spanked again?"

" 'Scuse me," said the Elephant's Child, "but I should not like it at all."

"How would you like to spank somebody?" said the Bi-Coloured-Python-Rock-Snake.

"I should like it very much indeed," said the Elephant's Child.

"Well," said the Bi-Coloured-Python-Rock-Snake, "you will find that new nose of yours very useful to spank people with."

"Thank you," said the Elephant's Child, "I 'll remember that; and now I think I 'll go home to all my dear families and try."

So the Elephant's Child went home across Africa frisking and whisking his trunk. When he wanted fruit to eat he

This is just a picture of the Elephant's Child going to pull bananas off
a banana-tree after he had got his fine new long trunk. I don't think it is
a very nice picture; but I could n't make it any better, because elephants
and bananas are hard to draw. The streaky things behind the Elephant's
Child mean squoggy marshy country somewhere in Africa. The Elephant's Child made most of his mud-cakes out of the mud that he found
there. I think it would look better if you painted the banana-tree green
and the Elephant's Child red.

29

pulled fruit down from a tree, instead of waiting for it to fall as he used to do. When he wanted grass he plucked grass up from the ground, instead of going on his knees as he used to do. When the flies bit him he broke off the branch of a tree

"He made himself a new, cool, slushy-squshy mud-cap whenever the sun was hot."

and used it as a fly-whisk; and he made himself a new, cool, slushy-squshy mud-cap whenever the sun was hot. When he felt lonely walking through Africa he sang to himself down his trunk, and the noise was louder than several brass bands. He went especially out of his way to find a broad Hippopotamus (she was no relation of his), and he spanked her very hard, to make sure that the Bi-Coloured-Python-Rock-Snake had spoken the truth about his new trunk. The rest of the time he picked up the melon rinds that he had dropped on his way to the Limpopo—for he was a Tidy Pachyderm.

One dark evening he came back to all his dear families, and he coiled up his trunk and said, "How do you do?" They were very glad to see him, and immediately said, "Come here and be spanked for your 'satiable curtiosity."

"Pooh," said the Elephant's Child. "I don't think you

peoples know anything about spanking; but *I* do, and I 'll show you."

Then he uncurled his trunk and knocked two of his dear brothers head over heels.

"O Bananas!" said they, "where did you learn that trick, and what have you done to your nose?"

"I got a new one from the Crocodile on the banks of the great, gray-green, greasy Limpopo River," said the Elephant's Child. "I asked him what he had for dinner, and he gave me this to keep."

"It looks very ugly," said his hairy uncle, the Baboon.

"It does," said the Elephant's Child. "But it 's very useful,"

"My trunk is ugly, but it 's very useful," said the Elephant's Child. And he picked up his hairy uncle by one hairy leg and hove him into a hornets' nest.

and he picked up his hairy uncle, the Baboon, by one hairy leg, and hove him into a hornets' nest.

Then that bad Elephant's Child spanked all his dear families for a long time, till they were very warm and greatly astonished. He pulled out his tall Ostrich aunt's tail-feathers; and he caught his tall uncle, the Giraffe, by the hindleg, and dragged him through a thorn-bush; and he shouted at his broad aunt, the Hippopotamus, and blew bubbles into her ear when she was sleeping in the water after meals; but he never let any one touch Kolokolo Bird.

At last things grew so exciting that his dear families went off one by one in a hurry to the banks of the great gray-green, greasy Limpopo River, all set about with fever-trees, to borrow new noses from the Crocodile. When they came back nobody spanked anybody any more; and ever since that day, O Best Beloved, all the Elephants you will ever see, besides all those that you won't, have trunks precisely like the trunk of the 'satiable Elephant's Child.

II

HOW THE CAMEL GOT HIS HUMP

From *Just So Stories*

Now this is the next tale, and it tells how the Camel got his big hump.

In the beginning of years, when the world was so new-and-all, and the Animals were just beginning to work for Man, there was a Camel, and he lived in the middle of a Howling Desert because he did not want to work; and besides, he was a Howler himself. So he ate sticks and thorns and tamarisks and milkweed and prickles, most 'scruciating idle; and when anybody spoke to him he said "Humph!" Just "Humph!" and no more.

Presently the Horse came to him on Monday morning, with a saddle on his back and a bit in his mouth, and said, "Camel, O Camel, come out and trot like the rest of us."

"Humph!" said the Camel; and the Horse went away and told the Man.

Presently the Dog came to him, with a stick in his mouth, and said, "Camel, O Camel, come and fetch and carry like the rest of us."

This is the picture of the Djinn making the beginnings of the Magic that brought the Humph to the Camel. First he drew a line in the air with his finger, and it became solid; and then he made a cloud, and then he made an egg—you can see them both at the bottom of the picture— and then there was a magic pumpkin that turned into a big white flame. Then the Djinn took his magic fan and fanned that flame till the flame turned into a magic by itself. It was a good Magic and a very kind Magic really, though it had to give the Camel a Humph because the Camel was lazy. The Djinn in charge of All Deserts was one of the nicest of the Djinns, so he would never do anything really unkind.

"Humph!" said the Camel; and the Dog went away and told the Man.

Presently the Ox came to him, with the yoke on his neck and said, "Camel, O Camel, come and plough like the rest of us."

"Humph!" said the Camel; and the Ox went away and told the Man.

At the end of the day the Man called the Horse and the Dog and the Ox together, and said, "Three, O Three, I 'm very sorry for you (with the world so new-and-all) ; but that Humph-thing in the Desert can't work, or he would have been here by now, so I am going to leave him alone, and you must work double time to make up for it."

That made the Three very angry (with the world so new-and-all), and they held a palaver, and an *ndaba* and a *punchayet*, and a pow-wow on the edge of the Desert; and the Camel came chewing milkweed *most* 'scruciating idle, and laughed at them. Then he said "Humph!" and went away again.

Presently there came along the Djinn in charge of All Deserts, rolling in a cloud of dust (Djinns always travel that way because it is Magic), and he stopped to palaver and pow-wow with the Three.

"Djinn of All Deserts," said the Horse, "*is* it right for any one to be idle, with the world so new-and-all?"

"Certainly not," said the Djinn.

"Well," said the Horse, "there 's a thing in the middle of your Howling Desert (and he 's a Howler himself) with a long neck and long legs, and he has n't done a stroke of work since Monday morning. He won't trot."

"Whew!" said the Djinn, whistling, "that 's my Camel, for all the gold in Arabia! What does he say about it?"

Here is the picture of the Djinn in charge of All Deserts guiding the Magic with his magic fan. The Camel is eating a twig of acacia, and he has just finished saying "humph" once too often (the Djinn told him he would), and so the Humph is coming. The long towelly-thing growing out of the thing like an onion is the Magic, and you can see the Humph on its shoulder. The Humph fits on the flat part of the Camel's back. The Camel is too busy looking at his own beautiful self in the pool of water to know what is going to happen to him.

"He says 'Humph!' " said the Dog; "and he won't fetch and carry."

"Does he say anything else?"

"Only 'Humph'; and he won't plough," said the Ox.

"Very good," said the Djinn. "I'll humph him if you will kindly wait a minute."

The Djinn rolled himself up in his dust-cloak, and took a bearing across the desert, and found the Camel most 'scruciatingly idle, looking at his own reflection in a pool of water.

"My long and bubbling friend," said the Djinn, "what's this I hear of your doing no work, with the world so new-and-all?"

"Humph!" said the Camel.

The Djinn sat down, with his chin in his hand, and began to think a Great Magic, while the Camel looked at his own reflection in the pool of water.

"You've given the Three extra work ever since Monday morning, all on account of your 'scruciating idleness," said the Djinn; and he went on thinking Magics, with his chin in his hand.

"Humph!" said the Camel.

"I shouldn't say that again if I were you," said the Djinn; "you might say it once too often. Bubbles, I want you to work."

And the Camel said "Humph!" again; but no sooner had he said it than he saw his back, that he was so proud of, puffing up and puffing up into a great big lolloping humph.

Underneath the truly picture is a picture of the World so new-and-all. There are two smoky volcanoes in it, some other mountains and some stones and a lake and a black island and a twisty river and a lot of other things, as well as a Noah's Ark. I couldn't draw all the deserts that the Djinn was in charge of, so I only drew one, but it is a most deserty desert.

"Do you see that?" said the Djinn. "That's your very own humph that you 've brought upon your very own self by not working. To-day is Thursday, and you 've done no work since Monday, when the work began. Now you are going to work."

"How can I," said the Camel, "with this humph on my back?"

"That's made a-purpose," said the Djinn, "all because you missed those three days. You will be able to work now for three days without eating, because you can live on your humph; and don't you ever say I never did anything for you. Come out of the Desert and go to the Three, and behave. Humph yourself!"

And the Camel humphed himself, humph and all, and went away to join the Three. And from that day to this the Camel always wears a humph (we call it "hump" now, not to hurt his feelings) ; but he has never yet caught up with the three days that he missed at the beginning of the world, and he has never yet learned how to behave.

> The Camel's hump is an ugly lump
>   Which well you may see at the Zoo;
> But uglier yet is the hump we get
>   From having too little to do.
>
> Kiddies and grown-ups too-oo-oo,
> If we have n't enough to do-oo-oo,
>   We get the hump—
>   Cameelious hump—
> The hump that is black and blue!
>
> We climb out of bed with a frouzly head
>   And a snarly-yarly voice.
> We shiver and scowl and we grunt and we growl
>   At our bath and our boots and our toys;

And there ought to be a corner for me
(And I know there is one for you)
When we get the hump—
Cameelious hump—
The hump that is black and blue!

The cure for this ill is not to sit still,
Or frowst with a book by the fire;
But to take a large hoe and a shovel also,
And dig till you gently perspire;

And then you will find that the sun and the wind,
And the Djinn of the Garden too,
Have lifted the hump—
The horrible hump—
The hump that is black and blue!

I get it as well as you-oo-oo—
If I have n't enough to do-oo-oo—
We all get hump—
Cameelious hump—
Kiddies and grown-ups too!

III

THE CAT THAT WALKED BY HIMSELF

From *Just So Stories*

Hear and attend and listen; for this befell and be-happened and became and was, O my Best Beloved, when the Tame animals were wild. The Dog was wild, and the Horse was wild, and the Cow was wild, and the Sheep was wild, and the Pig was wild—as wild as wild as could be—and they walked in the Wet Wild Woods by their wild lones. But the wildest of all the wild animals was the Cat. He walked by himself, and all places were alike to him.

Of course the Man was wild too. He was dreadfully wild. He did n't even begin to be tame till he met the Woman, and she told him that she did not like living in his wild ways. She picked out a nice dry Cave, instead of a heap of wet leaves, to lie down in; and she strewed clean sand on the floor; and she lit a nice fire of wood at the back of the Cave; and she hung a dried wild-horse skin, tail down, across the opening of the Cave; and she said, "Wipe your feet, dear, when you come in, and now we 'll keep house."

That night, Best Beloved, they ate wild sheep roasted on

the hot stones, and flavoured with wild garlic and wild pepper; and wild duck stuffed with wild rice and wild fenugreek and wild coriander; and marrow-bones of wild oxen; and wild cherries, and wild grenadillas. Then the Man went to sleep in front of the fire ever so happy; but the Woman sat up, combing her hair. She took the bone of the shoulder of mutton—the big fat blade-bone—and she looked at the wonderful marks on it, and she threw more wood on the fire, and she made a Magic. She made the First Singing Magic in the world.

Out in the Wet Wild Woods all the wild animals gathered together where they could see the light of the fire a long way off, and they wondered what it meant.

Then Wild Horse stamped with his wild foot and said, "O my Friends and O my Enemies, why have the Man and the Woman made that great light in that great Cave, and what harm will it do us?"

Wild Dog lifted up his wild nose and smelled the smell of roast mutton, and said, "I will go up and see and look, and say; for I think it is good. Cat, come with me."

"Nenni!" said the Cat. "I am the Cat who walks by himself, and all places are alike to me. I will not come."

"Then we can never be friends again," said Wild Dog, and he trotted off to the Cave. But when he had gone a little way the Cat said to himself, "All places are alike to me. Why should I not go too and see and look and come away at my own liking." So he slipped after Wild Dog softly, very softly, and hid himself where he could hear everything.

When Wild Dog reached the mouth of the Cave he lifted up the dried horse-skin with his nose and sniffed the beautiful smell of the roast mutton, and the Woman, looking at the blade-bone, heard him, and laughed, and said, "Here comes

This is the picture of the Cave where the Man and the Woman lived first of all. It was really a very nice Cave, and much warmer than it looks. The Man had a canoe. It is on the edge of the river, being soaked in the water to make it swell up. The tattery-looking thing across the river is the Man's salmon-net to catch salmon with. There are nice clean stones leading up from the river to the mouth of the Cave, so that the Man and the Woman could go down for water without getting sand between their toes. The things like black-beetles far down the beach are the first. Wild Thing out of the Wild Woods, what do you want?"

Wild Dog said, "O my Enemy and Wife of my Enemy, what is this that smells so good in the Wild Woods?"

Then the Woman picked up a roasted mutton-bone and threw it to Wild Dog, and said, "Wild Thing out of the Wild Woods, taste and try." Wild Dog gnawed the bone, and it was more delicious than anything he had ever tasted, and he said, "O my Enemy and Wife of my Enemy, give me another."

The Woman said, "Wild Thing out of the Wild Woods, help my Man to hunt through the day and guard this Cave at night, and I will give you as many roast bones as you need."

"Ah!" said the Cat, listening. "This is a very wise Woman, but she is not so wise as I am."

Wild Dog crawled into the Cave and laid his head on the Woman's lap, and said, "O my Friend and Wife of my Friend, I will help your Man to hunt through the day, and at night I will guard your Cave."

"Ah!" said the Cat, listening. "That is a very foolish Dog." And he went back through the Wet Wild Woods waving his wild tail, and walking by his wild lone. But he never told anybody.

---

really trunks of dead trees that floated down the river from the Wet Wild Woods on the other bank. The Man and the Woman used to drag them out and dry them and cut them up for firewood. I have n't drawn the horse-hide curtain at the mouth of the Cave, because the Woman has just taken it down to be cleaned. All those little smudges on the sand between the Cave and the river are the marks of the Woman's feet and the Man's feet.

The Man and the Woman are both inside the Cave eating their dinner.

They went to another cosier Cave when the Baby came, because the Baby used to crawl down to the river and fall in, and the Dog had to pull him out.

When the Man waked up he said, "What is Wild Dog doing here?" And the Woman said, "His name is not Wild Dog any more, but the First Friend, because he will be our friend for always and always and always. Take him with you when you go hunting."

Next night the Woman cut great green armfuls of fresh grass from the water-meadows, and dried it before the fire, so that it smelt like new-mown hay, and she sat at the mouth of the Cave and plaited a halter out of horse-hide, and she looked at the shoulder of mutton-bone—at the big broad blade-bone—and she made a Magic. She made the Second Singing Magic in the world.

Out in the Wild Woods all the wild animals wondered what had happened to Wild Dog, and at last Wild Horse stamped with his foot and said, "I will go and see and say why Wild Dog has not returned. Cat, come with me."

"Nenni!" said the Cat. "I am the Cat who walks by himself, and all places are alike to me. I will not come." But all the same he followed Wild Horse softly, very softly, and hid himself where he could hear everything.

When the Woman heard Wild Horse tripping and stumbling on his long mane, she laughed and said, "Here comes the second. Wild Thing out of the Wild Woods what do you want?"

Wild Horse said, "O my Enemy and Wife of my Enemy, where is Wild Dog?"

The Woman laughed, and picked up the blade-bone and looked at it, and said, "Wild Thing out of the Wild Woods, you did not come here for Wild Dog, but for the sake of this good grass."

And Wild Horse, tripping and stumbling on his long mane, said, "That is true; give it me to eat."

The Woman said, "Wild Thing out of the Wild Woods,

bend your wild head and wear what I give you, and you shall eat the wonderful grass three times a day."

"Ah," said the Cat, listening, "this is a clever Woman, but she is not so clever as I am."

Wild Horse bent his wild head, and the Woman slipped the plaited hide halter over it, and Wild Horse breathed on the Woman's feet and said, "O my Mistress, and Wife of my Master, I will be your servant for the sake of the wonderful grass."

"Ah," said the Cat, listening, "that is a very foolish Horse." And he went back through the Wet Wild Woods, waving his wild tail and walking by his wild lone. But he never told anybody.

When the Man and the Dog came back from hunting, the Man said, "What is Wild Horse doing here?" And the Woman said, "His name is not Wild Horse any more, but the First Servant, because he will carry us from place to place for always and always and always. Ride on his back when you go hunting."

Next day, holding her wild head high that her wild horns should not catch in the wild trees, Wild Cow came up to the Cave, and the Cat followed, and hid himself just the same as before; and everything happened just the same as before; and the Cat said the same things as before, and when Wild Cow had promised to give her milk to the Woman every day in exchange for the wonderful grass, the Cat went back through the Wet Wild Woods waving his wild tail and walking by his wild lone, just the same as before. But he never told anybody. And when the Man and the Horse and the Dog came home from hunting and asked the same questions same as before, the Woman said, "Her name is not Wild Cow any more, but the Giver of Good Food. She will give us the warm white milk for always and always and always, and I will take

This is the picture of the Cat that Walked by Himself, walking by his wild lone through the Wet Wild Woods and waving his wild tail. There is nothing else in the picture except some toadstools. They had to grow there because the woods were so wet. The lumpy thing on the low

care of her while you and the First Friend and the First
Servant go hunting."

Next day the Cat waited to see if any other Wild thing
would go up to the Cave, but no one moved in the Wet
Wild Woods, so the Cat walked there by himself; and he saw
the Woman milking the Cow, and he saw the light of the fire
in the Cave, and he smelt the smell of the warm white milk.

Cat said, "O my Enemy, and Wife of my Enemy, where
did Wild Cow go?"

The Woman laughed and said, "Wild Thing out of the
Wild Woods, go back to the Woods again, for I have braided
up my hair, and I have put away the magic blade-bone, and
we have no more need of either friends or servants in our
Cave."

Cat said, "I am not a friend, and I am not a servant. I am
the Cat who walks by himself, and I wish to come into your
cave."

Woman said, "Then why did you not come with First
Friend on the first night?"

Cat grew very angry and said, "Has Wild Dog told tales
of me?"

Then the Woman laughed and said, "You are the Cat who
walks by himself, and all places are alike to you. You are
neither a friend nor a servant. You have said it yourself. Go
away and walk by yourself in all places alike."

Then Cat pretended to be sorry and said, "Must I never

---

branch is n't a bird. It is moss that grew there because the Wild Woods
were so wet.

Underneath the truly picture is a picture of the cosy Cave that the
Man and the Woman went to after the Baby came. It was their summer
Cave, and they planted wheat in front of it. The Man is riding on the
Horse to find the Cow and bring her back to the Cave to be milked. He
is holding up his hand to call the Dog, who has swum across to the other
side of the river, looking for rabbits.

come into the Cave? Must I never sit by the warm fire? Must I never drink the warm white milk? You are very wise and very beautiful. You should not be cruel even to a Cat."

Woman said, "I knew I was wise, but I did not know I was beautiful. So I will make a bargain with you. If ever I say one word in your praise you may come into the Cave."

"And if you say two words in my praise?" said the Cat.

"I never shall," said the Woman, "but if I say two words in your praise, you may sit by the fire in the Cave."

"And if you say three words?" said the Cat.

"I never shall," said the Woman, "but if I say three words in your praise, you may drink the warm white milk three times a day for always and always and always."

Then the Cat arched his back and said, "Now let the Curtain at the mouth of the Cave, and the Fire at the back of the Cave, and the Milk-pots that stand beside the Fire, remember what my Enemy and the Wife of my Enemy has said." And he went away through the Wet Wild Woods waving his wild tail and walking by his wild lone.

That night when the Man and the Horse and the Dog came home from hunting, the Woman did not tell them of the bargain that she had made with the Cat, because she was afraid that they might not like it.

Cat went far and far away and hid himself in the Wet Wild Woods by his wild lone for a long time till the Woman forgot all about him. Only the Bat—the little upside-down Bat—that hung inside the Cave, knew where Cat hid; and every evening Bat would fly to Cat with news of what was happening.

One evening Bat said, "There is a Baby in the Cave. He is new and pink and fat and small, and the Woman is very fond of him."

"Ah," said the Cat, listening, "but what is the Baby fond of?"

"He is fond of things that are soft and tickle," said the Bat. "He is fond of warm things to hold in his arms when he goes to sleep. He is fond of being played with. He is fond of all those things."

"Ah," said the Cat, listening, "then my time has come."

Next night Cat walked through the Wet Wild Woods and hid very near the Cave till morning-time, and Man and Dog and Horse went hunting. The Woman was busy cooking that morning, and the Baby cried and interrupted. So she carried him outside the Cave and gave him a handful of pebbles to play with. But still the Baby cried.

Then the Cat put out his paddy paw and patted the Baby on the cheek, and it cooed; and the Cat rubbed against its fat knees and tickled it under its fat chin with his tail. And the Baby laughed; and the Woman heard him and smiled.

Then the Bat—the little upside-down Bat—that hung in the mouth of the Cave said, "O my Hostess and Wife of my Host and Mother of my Host's Son, a Wild Thing from the Wild Woods is most beautifully playing with your Baby."

"A blessing on that Wild Thing whoever he may be," said the Woman, straightening her back, "for I was a busy woman this morning and he has done me a service."

The very minute and second, Best Beloved, the dried horse-skin Curtain that was stretched tail-down at the mouth of the Cave fell down—*woosh!*—because it remembered the bargain she had made with the Cat, and when the Woman went to pick it up—lo and behold!—the Cat was sitting quite comfy inside the Cave.

"O my Enemy and Wife of my Enemy and Mother of my Enemy," said the Cat, "it is I; for you have spoken a word in my praise, and now I can sit within the Cave for always and always and always. But still I am the Cat who walks by himself, and all places are alike to me."

The Woman was very angry, and shut her lips tight and took up her spinning-wheel and began to spin.

But the Baby cried because the Cat had gone away, and the Woman could not hush it, for it struggled and kicked and grew black in the face.

"O my Enemy and Wife of my Enemy and Mother of my Enemy," said the Cat, "take a strand of the wire that you are spinning and tie it to your spinning-whorl and drag it along the floor, and I will show you a magic that shall make your Baby laugh as loudly as he is now crying."

"I will do so," said the Woman, "because I am at my wits' end; but I will not thank you for it."

She tied the thread to the little clay spindle-whorl and drew it across the floor, and the Cat ran after it and patted it with his paws and rolled head over heels, and tossed it backward over his shoulder and chased it between his hind legs and pretended to lose it, and pounced down upon it again, till the Baby laughed as loudly as it had been crying, and scrambled after the Cat and frolicked all over the Cave till it grew tired and settled down to sleep with the Cat in its arms.

"Now," said the Cat, "I will sing the Baby a song that shall keep him asleep for an hour." And he began to purr, loud and low, low and loud, till the Baby fell fast asleep. The Woman smiled as she looked down upon the two of them and said, "That was wonderfully done. No question but you are very clever, O Cat."

That very minute and second, Best Beloved, the smoke of the fire at the back of the Cave came down in clouds from the roof—*puff!*—because it remembered the bargain she had made with the Cat, and when it had cleared away—lo, and behold!—the Cat was sitting quite comfy close to the fire.

"O my Enemy and Wife of my Enemy and Mother of my Enemy," said the Cat, "it is I; for you have spoken a second word in my praise, and now I can sit by the warm fire at the back of the Cave for always and always and always. But still I am the Cat who walks by himself, and all places are alike to me."

Then the Woman was very, very angry, and let down her hair and put more wood on the fire, and brought out the broad blade-bone of the shoulder of mutton and began to make a Magic that should prevent her from saying a third word in praise of the Cat. It was not a Singing Magic, Best Beloved, it was a Still Magic; and by and by the Cave grew so still that a little wee-wee mouse crept out of a corner and ran across the floor.

"O my Enemy and Wife of my Enemy and Mother of my Enemy," said the Cat, "is that little mouse part of your magic?"

"Ouh! Chee! No indeed!" said the Woman, and she dropped the blade-bone and jumped upon the footstool in front of the fire and braided up her hair very quick for fear that the mouse should run up it.

"Ah," said the Cat, watching, "then the mouse will do me no harm if I eat it?"

"No," said the Woman, braiding up her hair, "eat it quickly and I will ever be grateful to you."

Cat made one jump and caught the little mouse, and the Woman said, "A hundred thanks. Even the First Friend is not quick enough to catch little mice as you have done. You must be very wise."

That very moment and second, O Best Beloved, the Milk-pot that stood by the fire cracked in two pieces—*ffft*—because it remembered the bargain she had made with the Cat, and when the Woman jumped down from the footstool—lo and behold!—the Cat was lapping up the warm white milk that lay in one of the broken pieces.

"O my Enemy and Wife of my Enemy and Mother of my Enemy," said the Cat, "it is I; for you have spoken three words in my praise, and now I can drink the warm white milk three times a day for always and always and always. But *still* I am the Cat who walks by himself, and all places are alike to me."

Then the Woman laughed and set the Cat a bowl of the warm white milk and said, "O Cat, you are as clever as a man, but remember that your bargain was not made with the Man or the Dog, and I do not know what they will do when they come home."

"What is that to me?" said the Cat. "If I have my place in the Cave by the fire and my warm white milk three times a day I do not care what the Man or the Dog can do."

That evening when the Man and the Dog came into the Cave, the Woman told them all the story of the bargain while the Cat sat by the fire and smiled. Then the Man said, "Yes, but he has not made a bargain with *me* or with all proper Men after me." Then he took off his two leather boots and he took up his little stone axe (that makes three) and he fetched a piece of wood and a hatchet (that is five altogether), and he set them out in a row and he said, "Now we will make *our* bargain. If you do not catch mice when you are in the Cave for always and always and always, I will throw these five things at you whenever I see you, and so shall all proper Men do after me."

"Ah," said the Woman, listening, "this is a very clever Cat, but he is not so clever as my Man."

The Cat counted the five things (and they looked very knobby) and he said, "I will catch mice when I am in the Cave for always and always and always; but *still* I am the Cat who walks by himself, and all places are alike to me."

"Not when I am near," said the Man. "If you had not said that last I would have put all these things away for always and always and always; but I am now going to throw my two boots and my little stone axe (that makes three) at you whenever I meet you. And so shall all proper Men do after me!"

Then the Dog said, "Wait a minute. He has not made a bargain with *me* or with all proper Dogs after me." And he showed his teeth and said, "If you are not kind to the Baby while I am in the Cave for always and always and always, I will hunt you till I catch you, and when I catch you I will bite you. And so shall all proper Dogs do after me."

"Ah," said the Woman, listening, "this is a very clever Cat, but he is not so clever as the Dog."

Cat counted the Dog's teeth (and they looked very pointed) and he said, "I will be kind to the Baby while I am in the Cave, as long as he does not pull my tail too hard, for always and always and always. But *still* I am the Cat that walks by himself, and all places are alike to me."

"Not when I am near," said the Dog. "If you had not said that last I would have shut my mouth for always and always and always; but *now* I am going to hunt you up a tree whenever I meet you. And so shall all proper Dogs do after me."

Then the Man threw his two boots and his little stone axe (that makes three) at the Cat, and the Cat ran out of the Cave and the Dog chased him up a tree; and from that day to this, Best Beloved, three proper Men out of five will always throw things at a Cat whenever they meet him, and all proper Dogs will chase him up a tree. But the Cat keeps his side of the bargain too. He will kill mice and he will be kind to Babies when he is in the house, just as long as they do not pull his tail too hard. But when he has done that, and between times, and when the moon gets up and night comes, he is the Cat that walks by himself, and all places are alike to him.

Then he goes out to the Wet Wild Woods or up the Wet Wild Trees or on the Wet Wild Roofs, waving his wild tail and walking by his wild lone.

IV

THE BEGINNING OF THE ARMADILLOS

From *Just So Stories*

THIS, O Best Beloved, is another story of the High and Far-Off Times. In the very middle of those times was a Stickly-Prickly Hedgehog, and he lived on the banks of the turbid Amazon, eating shelly snails and things. And he had a friend, a Slow-Solid Tortoise, who lived on the banks of the turbid Amazon, eating green lettuces and things. And so *that* was all right, Best Beloved. Do you see?

But also, and at the same time, in those High and Far-Off Times, there was a Painted Jaguar, and he lived on the banks of the turbid Amazon too; and he ate everything that he could catch. When he could not catch deer or monkeys he would eat frogs and beetles; and when he could not catch frogs and beetles he went to his Mother Jaguar, and she told him how to eat hedgehogs and tortoises.

She said to him ever so many times, graciously waving her tail, "My son, when you find a Hedgehog you must drop him into the water and then he will uncoil, and when you catch a Tortoise you must scoop him out of his shell with your paw." And so that was all right, Best Beloved.

One beautiful night on the banks of the turbid Amazon, Painted Jaguar found Stickly-Prickly Hedgehog and Slow-Solid Tortoise sitting under the trunk of a fallen tree. They could not run away, and so Stickly-Prickly curled himself up into a ball, because he was a Hedgehog, and Slow-Solid Tortoise drew in his head and feet into his shell as far as they would go, because he was a Tortoise; and so *that* was all right, Best Beloved. Do you see?

"Now attend to me," said Painted Jaguar, "because this is very important. My mother said that when I meet a Hedgehog I am to drop him into the water and then he will uncoil, and when I meet a Tortoise I am to scoop him out of his shell with my paw. Now which of you is Hedgehog and which is Tortoise? because to save my spots, I can't tell."

"Are you sure of what your Mummy told you?" said Stickly-Prickly Hedgehog. "Are you quite sure? Perhaps she said that when you uncoil a Tortoise you must shell him out of the water with a scoop, and when you paw a Hedgehog you must drop him on the shell."

"Are you sure of what your Mummy told you?" said Slow-and-Solid Tortoise. "Are you quite sure? Perhaps she said that when you water a Hedgehog you must drop him into your paw, and when you meet a Tortoise you must shell him till he uncoils."

"I don't think it was at all like that," said Painted Jaguar, but he felt a little puzzled; "but, please say it again more distinctly."

"When you scoop water with your paw you uncoil it with a Hedgehog," said Stickly-Prickly. "Remember that, because it 's important."

"*But,*" said the Tortoise, "when you paw your meat you drop it into a Tortoise with a scoop. Why can't you understand?"

"You are making my spots ache," said Painted Jaguar; "and besides, I did n't want your advice at all. I only wanted to know which of you is Hedgehog and which is Tortoise."

"I shan't tell you," said Stickly-Prickly; "but you can scoop me out of my shell if you like."

"Aha!" said Painted Jaguar. "Now I know you 're Tortoise. You thought I would n't! Now I will." Painted Jaguar darted out his paddy-paw just as Stickly-Prickly curled himself up, and of course Jaguar's paddy-paw was just filled with prickles. Worse than that, he knocked Stickly-Prickly away and away into the woods and the bushes, where it was too dark to find him. Then he put his paddy-paw into his mouth, and of course the prickles hurt him worse than ever. As soon as he could speak he said, "Now I know he is n't Tortoise at all. But"—and then he scratched his head with his un-prickly paw—"how do I know that this other is Tortoise?"

"But I *am* Tortoise," said Slow-and-Solid. "Your mother was quite right. She said that you were to scoop me out of my shell with your paw. Begin."

"You did n't say she said that a minute ago," said Painted Jaguar, sucking the prickles out of his paddy-paw. "You said she said something quite different."

"Well, suppose you say that I said that she said something quite different, I don't see that it makes any difference; because if she said what you said I said she said, it 's just the same as if I said what she said she said. On the other hand, if you think she said that you were to uncoil me with a scoop, instead of pawing me into drops with a shell, I can't help that, can I?"

"But you said you wanted to be scooped out of your shell with my paw," said Painted Jaguar.

"If you 'll think again you 'll find that I did n't say anything of the kind. I said that your mother said that you were to scoop me out of my shell," said Slow-and-Solid.

"What will happen if I do?" said the Jaguar most sniffily and most cautious.

"I don't know, because I 've never been scooped out of my shell before; but I tell you truly, if you want to see me swim away you 've only got to drop me into the water."

"I don't believe it," said Painted Jaguar. "You 've mixed up all the things my mother told me to do with the things that you asked me whether I was sure that she did n't say, till I don't know whether I 'm on my head or my painted tail; and now you come and tell me something I *can* understand, and it makes me more mixy than before. My mother told me that I was to drop one of you two into the water, and as you seem so anxious to be dropped I think you don't want to be dropped. So jump into the turbid Amazon and be quick about it."

"I warn you that your Mummy won't be pleased. Don't tell her I did n't tell you," said Slow-and-Solid.

"If you say another word about what my mother said——" the Jaguar answered, but he had not finished the sentence before Slow-and-Solid quietly dived into the turbid Amazon, swam under water for a long way, and came out on the bank where Stickly-Prickly was waiting for him.

"That was a very narrow escape," said Stickly-Prickly. "I don't like Painted Jaguar. What did you tell him that you were?"

"I told him truthfully that I was a truthful Tortoise, but he would n't believe it, and he made me jump into the river to see if I was, and I was, and he is surprised. Now he 's gone to tell his Mummy. Listen to him!"

They could hear Painted Jaguar roaring up and down among the trees and the bushes by the side of the turbid Amazon, till his Mummy came.

"Son, son!" said his mother ever so many times, graciously waving her tail, "what have you been doing that you should n't have done?"

"I tried to scoop something that said it wanted to be scooped out of its shell with my paw, and my paw is full of per-ickles," said Painted Jaguar.

"Son, son!" said his mother ever so many times, graciously waving her tail, "by the prickles in your paddy-paw I see that that must have been a Hedgehog. You should have dropped him into the water."

"I did that to the other thing; and he said he was a Tortoise, and I did n't believe him, and it was quite true, and he has dived under the turbid Amazon, and he won't come up again, and I have n't anything at all to eat, and I think we had better find lodgings somewhere else. They are too clever on the turbid Amazon for poor me!"

"Son, son!" said his mother ever so many times, graciously waving her tail, "now attend to me and remember what I say. A hedgehog curls himself up into a ball and his prickles stick out every which way at once. By this you may know the Hedgehog."

"I don't like this old lady one little bit," said Stickly-Prickly, under the shadow of a large leaf. "I wonder what else she knows?"

"A Tortoise can't curl himself up," Mother Jaguar went on, ever so many times, graciously waving her tail. "He only draws his head and legs into his shell. By this you may know the Tortoise."

"I don't like this old lady at all—at all," said Slow-and-Solid Tortoise. "Even Painted Jaguar can't forget those directions. It 's a great pity that you can't swim, Stickly-Prickly."

"Don't talk to me," said Stickly-Prickly. "Just think how

much better it would be if you could curl up. This *is* a mess! Listen to Painted Jaguar."

Painted Jaguar was sitting on the banks of the turbid Amazon sucking prickles out of his paw and saying to himself—

> "Can't curl, but can swim—
> Slow-Solid, that 's him!
> Curls up, but can't swim—
> Stickly-Prickly, that 's him!"

"He 'll never forget that this month of Sundays," said Stickly-Prickly. "Hold up my chin, Slow-and-Solid. I 'm going to try to learn to swim. It may be useful."

"Excellent!" said Slow-and-Solid; and he held up Stickly-Prickly's chin, while Stickly-Prickly kicked in the waters of the turbid Amazon.

"You 'll make a fine swimmer yet," said Slow-and-Solid. "Now, if you can unlace my back-plates a little, I 'll see what I can do toward curling up. It may be useful."

Stickly-Prickly helped to unlace Tortoise's back-plates, so that by twisting and straining Slow-and-Solid actually managed to curl up a tiddy wee bit.

"Excellent!" said Stickly-Prickly; "but I should n't do any more just now. It 's making you black in the face. Kindly lead me into the water once again and I 'll practise that side-stroke which you say is so easy." And so Stickly-Prickly practised, and Slow-Solid swam alongside.

"Excellent!" said Slow-and-Solid. "A little more practice will make you a regular whale. Now, if I may trouble you to unlace my back and front plates two holes more, I 'll try that fascinating bend that you say is so easy. Won't Painted Jaguar be surprised!"

"Excellent!" said Stickly-Prickly, all wet from the turbid Amazon. "I declare I should n't know you from one of my own family. Two holes, I think you said? A little more expression, please, and don't grunt quite so much, or Painted Jaguar may hear us. When you 've finished, I want to try that long dive which you say is so easy. Won't Painted Jaguar be surprised!"

And so Stickly-Prickly dived, and Slow-and-Solid dived alongside.

"Excellent!" said Slow-and-Solid. "A leetle more attention to holding your breath and you will be able to keep house at the bottom of the turbid Amazon. Now I 'll try that exercise of wrapping my hind legs round my ears which you say is so peculiarly comfortable. Won't Painted Jaguar be surprised!"

"Excellent!" said Stickly-Prickly. "But it 's straining your back-plates a little. They are all overlapping now, instead of lying side by side."

"Oh, that 's the result of exercise," said Slow-and-Solid. "I 've noticed that your prickles seem to be melting into one another, and that you 're growing to look rather more like a pine-cone, and less like a chestnut-burr, than you used to."

"Am I?" said Stickly-Prickly. "That comes from my soaking in the water. Oh, won't Painted Jaguar be surprised!"

They went on with their exercises, each helping the other, till morning came; and when the sun was high they rested and dried themselves. Then they saw that they were both of them quite different from what they had been.

"Stickly-Prickly," said Tortoise after breakfast, "I am not what I was yesterday; but I think that I may yet amuse Painted Jaguar."

"That was the very thing I was thinking just now," said Stickly-Prickly. "I think scales are a tremendous improvement on prickles—to say nothing of being able to swim. Oh, *won't* Painted Jaguar be surprised! Let 's go and find him."

By and by they found Painted Jaguar, still nursing his

This is a picture of the whole story of the Jaguar and the Hedgehog and the Tortoise and the Armadillo all in a heap. It looks rather the same any way you turn it. The Tortoise is in the middle learning how to bend, and that is why the shelly plates on his back are so spread apart. He is standing on the Hedgehog, who is waiting to learn how to swim. The Hedgehog is a Japanesy Hedgehog, because I couldn't find our own hedgehogs in the garden when I wanted to draw them. (It was daytime, and they had gone to bed under the dahlias.) Speckly Jaguar is looking over the edge, with his paddy-paw carefully tied up by his mother, because he pricked himself scooping the Hedgehog. He is much surprised to see what the Tortoise is doing, and his paw is hurting him. The snouty thing with the little eye that Speckly Jaguar is trying to climb over is the Armadillo that the Tortoise and the Hedgehog are going to turn into when they have finished bending and swimming. It is all a magic picture, and that is one of the reasons why I haven't drawn the

paddy-paw that had been hurt the night before. He was so astonished that he fell three times backward over his own painted tail without stopping.

"Good morning!" said Stickly-Prickly. "And how is your dear gracious Mummy this morning?"

"She is quite well, thank you," said Painted Jaguar; "but you must forgive me if I do not at this precise moment recall your name."

"That's unkind of you," said Stickly-Prickly, "seeing that this time yesterday you tried to scoop me out of my shell with your paw."

"But you hadn't any shell. It was all prickles," said Painted Jaguar. "I know it was. Just look at my paw!"

"You told me to drop into the turbid Amazon and be drowned," said Slow-Solid. "Why are you so rude and forgetful to-day?"

"Don't you remember what your mother told you?" said Stickly-Prickly—

> "'Can't curl, but can swim—
> Stickly-Prickly, that's him!
> Curls up, but can't swim—
> Slow-Solid, that's him!'"

Then they both curled themselves up and rolled round and round Painted Jaguar till his eyes turned truly cartwheels in his head.

Then he went to fetch his mother.

"Mother," he said, "there are two new animals in the woods to-day, and the one that you said couldn't swim, swims, and the one that you said couldn't curl up, curls; and

---

Jaguar's whiskers. The other reason was that he was so young that his whiskers had not grown. The Jaguar's pet name with his Mummy was Doffles.

they 've gone shares in their prickles, I think, because both of them are scaly all over, instead of one being smooth and the other very prickly; and, besides that, they are rolling round and round in circles, and I don't feel comfy."

"Son, son!" said Mother Jaguar ever so many times, graciously waving her tail, "a Hedgehog is a Hedgehog, and can't be anything but a Hedgehog; and a Tortoise is a Tortoise, and can never be anything else."

"But it is n't a Hedgehog, and it is n't a Tortoise. It 's a little bit of both, and I don't know its proper name."

"Nonsense!" said Mother Jaguar. "Everything has its proper name. I should call it 'Armadillo' till I found out the real one. And I should leave it alone."

So Painted Jaguar did as he was told, especially about leaving them alone; but the curious thing is that from that day to this, O Best Beloved, no one on the banks of the turbid Amazon has ever called Stickly-Prickly and Slow-Solid anything except Armadillo. There are Hedgehogs and Tortoises in other places, of course (there are some in my garden); but the real old and clever kind, with their scales lying lippety-lappety one over the other, like pine-cone scales, that lived on the banks of the turbid Amazon in the High and Far-Off Days, are always called Armadillos, because they were so clever.

So *that* 's all right, Best Beloved. Do you see?

V

HOW THE RHINOCEROS GOT HIS SKIN
From *Just So Stories*

ONCE upon a time, on an uninhabited island on the shores of the Red Sea, there lived a Parsee from whose hat the rays of the sun were reflected in more-than-oriental splendour. And the Parsee lived by the Red Sea with nothing but his hat and his knife and a cooking-stove of the kind that you must particularly never touch. And one day he took flour and water and currants and plums and sugar and things, and made himself one cake which was two feet across and three feet thick. It was indeed a Superior Comestible (*that's* magic), and he put it on the stove because *he* was allowed to cook on that stove, and he baked it and he baked it till it was all done brown and smelt most sentimental. But just as he was going to eat it there came down to the beach from the Altogether Uninhabited Interior one Rhinoceros with a horn on his nose, two piggy eyes, and few manners. In those days the Rhinoceros's skin fitted him quite tight. There were not wrinkles in it anywhere. He looked exactly like a Noah's Ark Rhinoceros, but of course much bigger. All the

This is the picture of the Parsee beginning to eat his cake on the Uninhabited Island in the Red Sea on a very hot day; and of the Rhinoceros coming down from the Altogether Uninhabited Interior, which, as you can truthfully see, is all rocky. The Rhinoceros's skin is quite smooth, and the three buttons that button it up are underneath, so you can't see them. The squiggly things on the Parsee's hat are the rays of the sun reflected in more-than-oriental splendour, because if I had drawn real rays they would have filled up all the picture. The cake has currants in it; and the wheel-thing lying on the sand in front belonged to one of Pharaoh's chariots when he tried to cross the Red Sea. The Parsee found it, and kept it to play with. The Parsee's name was Pestonjee Bomonjee, and the Rhinoceros was called Strorks, because he breathed through his mouth instead of his nose. I would n't ask anything about the cooking-stove if I were you.

same, he had no manners then, and he has no manners now, and he never will have any manners. He said "How!" and the Parsee left that cake and climbed to the top of a palm-tree with nothing on but his hat, from which the rays of the sun were always reflected in more-than-oriental splendour. And the Rhinoceros upset the oil-stove with his nose, and the cake rolled on the sand, and he spiked that cake on the horn of his nose, and he ate it, and he went away, waving his tail, to the desolate and Exclusively Uninhabited Interior which abuts on the islands of Mazanderan, Socotra, and the Promontories of the Larger Equinox. Then the Parsee came down from his palm-tree and put the stove on its legs and recited the following *Sloka*, which, as you have not heard, I will now proceed to relate:—

> Them that takes cakes
> Which the Parsee-man bakes
> Makes dreadful mistakes.

And there was a great deal more in that than you would think.

Because, five weeks later, there was a heat-wave in the Red Sea, and everybody took off all the clothes they had. The Parsee took off his hat; but the Rhinoceros took off his skin and carried it over his shoulder as he came down to the beach to bathe. In those days it buttoned underneath with three buttons and looked like a waterproof. He said nothing whatever about the Parsee's cake, because he had eaten it all; and he never had any manners, then, since, or henceforward. He waddled straight into the water and blew bubbles through his nose, leaving his skin on the beach.

Presently the Parsee came by and found the skin, and he smiled one smile that ran all round his face two times. Then he danced three times round the skin and rubbed his hands.

Then he went to his camp and filled his hat with cake-crumbs, for the Parsee never ate anything but cake and never swept out his camp. He took that skin, and he shook that skin, and he scrubbed that skin, and he rubbed that skin just as full of old, dry, stale, tickly cake-crumbs and some burned currants as ever it could *possibly* hold. Then he climbed to the top of his palm-tree and waited for the Rhinoceros to come out of the water and put it on.

And the Rhinoceros did. He buttoned it up with the three buttons, and it tickled like cake-crumbs in bed. Then he wanted to scratch, but that made it worse; and then he lay down on the sands and rolled and rolled and rolled, and every time he rolled the cake-crumbs tickled him worse and worse and worse. Then he ran to the palm-tree and rubbed and rubbed and rubbed himself against it. He rubbed so much and so hard that he rubbed his skin into a great fold over his shoulders, and another fold underneath, where the buttons used to be (but he rubbed the buttons off), and he rubbed some more folds over his legs. And it spoiled his temper, but it did n't make the least difference to the cake-crumbs. They

---

This is the Parsee Pestonjee Bomonjee sitting in his palm-tree and watching the Rhinoceros Strorks bathing near the beach of the Altogether Uninhabited Island after Strorks had taken off his skin. The Parsee has put the cake-crumbs into the skin, and he is smiling to think how they will tickle Strorks when Strorks puts it on again. The skin is just under the rocks below the palm-tree in a cool place; that is why you can't see it. The Parsee is wearing a new more-than-oriental splendour hat of the sort that Parsees wear; and he has a knife in his hand to cut his name on palm-trees. The black things on the islands out at sea are bits of ships that got wrecked going down the Red Sea; but all the passengers were saved and went home.

The black thing in the water close to the shore is not a wreck at all. It is Strorks the Rhinoceros bathing without his skin. He was just as black underneath his skin as he was outside. I wouldn't ask anything about the cooking-stove if I were you.

were inside his skin and they tickled. So he went home, very angry indeed and horribly scratchy; and from that day to this every rhinoceros has great folds in his skin and a very bad temper, all on account of the cake-crumbs inside.

But the Parsee came down from his palm-tree, wearing his hat, from which the rays of the sun were reflected in more-than-oriental splendour, packed up his cooking-stove, and went away in the direction of Orotavo, Amygdala, the Upland Meadows of Anantarivo, and the Marshes of Sonaput.

VI

THE SING–SONG OF OLD MAN KANGAROO

From *Just So Stories*

Not always was the Kangaroo as now we do behold him, but a Different Animal with four short legs. He was gray and he was woolly, and his pride was inordinate: he danced on an outcrop in the middle of Australia, and he went to the Little God Nqa at six before breakfast, saying, "Make me different from all other animals by five this afternoon."

Up jumped Nqa from his seat on the sandflat and shouted, "Go away!"

He was gray and he was woolly, and his pride was inordinate: he danced on a rockledge in the middle of Australia, and he went to the Middle God Nquing.

He went to Nquing at eight after breakfast, saying, "Make me different from all other animals; make me, also, wonderfully popular by five this afternoon."

Up jumped Nquing from his burrow in the spinifex and shouted, "Go away!"

He was gray and he was woolly, and his pride was inordinate: he danced on a sandbank in the middle of Australia, and he went to the Big God Nqong.

    This is a picture of Old Man Kangaroo when he was the Different Animal with four short legs. I have drawn him gray and woolly, and you can see that he is very proud because he has a wreath of flowers in his hair. He is dancing on an outcrop (that means a ledge of rock) in the middle of Australia at six o'clock before breakfast. You can see that it is six o'clock, because the sun is just getting up. The thing with the ears and the open mouth is Little God Nqa. Nqa is very much surprised, because he has never seen a Kangaroo dance like that before. Little God Nqa is just saying, "Go away," but the Kangaroo is so busy dancing that he has not heard him yet.

    The Kangaroo hasn't any real name except Boomer. He lost it because he was so proud.

He went to Nqong at ten before dinner-time, saying, "Make me different from all other animals; make me popular and wonderfully run after by five this afternoon."

Up jumped Nqong from his bath in the salt-pan and shouted, "Yes, I will!"

Nqong called Dingo—Yellow-Dog Dingo—always hungry, dusty in the sunshine, and showed him Kangaroo. Nqong said, "Dingo! Wake up, Dingo! Do you see that gentleman dancing on an ash-pit? He wants to be popular and very truly run after. Dingo, make him so!"

Up jumped Dingo—Yellow-Dog Dingo—and said, "What, *that* cat-rabbit?"

Off ran Dingo—Yellow-Dog Dingo—always hungry, grinning like a coal-scuttle—ran after Kangaroo.

Off went the proud Kangaroo on his four little legs like a bunny.

This, O Beloved of mine, ends the first part of the tale!

He ran through the desert; he ran through the mountains; he ran through the salt-pans; he ran through the reed-beds; he ran through the blue gums; he ran through the spinifex; he ran till his front legs ached.

He had to!

Still ran Dingo—Yellow-Dog Dingo—always hungry, grinning like a rat-trap, never getting nearer, never getting farther—ran after Kangaroo.

He had to!

Still ran Kangaroo—Old Man Kangaroo. He ran through the ti-trees; he ran through the mulga; he ran through the long grass; he ran through the short grass; he ran through the Tropics of Capricorn and Cancer; he ran till his hind legs ached.

He had to!

Still ran Dingo—Yellow-Dog Dingo—hungrier and hun-

This is the picture of Old Man Kangaroo at five in the afternoon, when he had got his beautiful hind legs just as Big God Nqong had promised. You can see that it is five o'clock, because Big God Nqong's pet tame clock says so. That is Nqong in his bath, sticking his feet out. Old Man Kangaroo is being rude to Yellow-Dog Dingo. Yellow-Dog Dingo has been trying to catch Kangaroo all across Australia. You can see the marks of Kangaroo's big new feet running ever so far back over the bare hills. Yellow-Dog Dingo is drawn black, because I am not allowed to paint these pictures with real colours out of the paint-box; and besides, Yellow-Dog Dingo got dreadfully black and dusty after running through the Flinders and the Cinders.

I don't know the names of the flowers growing round Nqong's bath. The two little squatty things out in the desert are the other two gods that Old Man Kangaroo spoke to early in the morning. That thing with grier, grinning like a horse-collar, never getting nearer, never getting farther; and they came to the Wollgong River.

Now, there was n't any bridge, and there was n't any ferry-boat, and Kangaroo did n't know how to get over; so he stood on his legs and hopped.

He had to!

He hopped through the Flinders; he hopped through the Cinders; he hopped through the deserts in the middle of Australia. He hopped like a Kangaroo.

First he hopped one yard; then he hopped three yards; then he hopped five yards; his legs growing stronger; his legs growing longer. He had n't any time for rest or refreshment, and he wanted them very much.

Still ran Dingo—Yellow-Dog Dingo—very much bewildered, very much hungry, and wondering what in the world or out of it made Old Man Kangaroo hop.

For he hopped like a cricket; like a pea in a sauce-pan; or a new rubber ball on a nursery floor.

He had to!

He tucked up his front legs; he hopped on his hind legs; he stuck out his tail for a balance-weight behind him; and he hopped through the Darling Downs.

He had to!

Still ran Dingo—Tired Dog Dingo—hungrier and hungrier, very much bewildered, and wondering when in the world or out of it would Old Man Kangaroo stop.

Then came Nqong from his bath in the salt-pan, and said, "It 's five o'clock."

Down sat Dingo—Poor Dog Dingo—always hungry, dusky in the sunshine; hung out his tongue and howled.

the letters on it is Old Man Kangaroo's pouch. He had to have a pouch just as he had to have legs.

Down sat Kangaroo—Old Man Kangaroo—stuck out his tail like a milking-stool behind him, and said, "Thank goodness *that's* finished!"

Then said Nqong, who is always a gentleman, "Why are n't you grateful to Yellow-Dog Dingo? Why don't you thank him for all he has done for you?"

Then said Kangaroo—Tired Old Kangaroo—"He's chased me out of the homes of my childhood; he 's chased me out of my regular meal-times; he 's altered my shape so I 'll never get it back; and he 's played Old Scratch with my legs."

Then said Nqong, "Perhaps I 'm mistaken, but didn't you ask me to make you different from all other animals, as well as to make you very truly sought after? And now it is five o'clock."

"Yes," said Kangaroo. "I wish that I had n't. I thought you would do it by charms and incantations, but this is a practical joke."

"Joke!" said Nqong from his bath in the blue gums. "Say that again and I 'll whistle up Dingo and run your hind legs off."

"No," said the Kangaroo. "I must apologize. Legs are legs, and you need n't alter 'em so far as I am concerned. I only meant to explain to Your Lordliness that I 've had nothing to eat since morning, and I 'm very empty indeed."

"Yes," said Dingo—Yellow-Dog Dingo—"I am just in the same situation. I 've made him different from all other animals; but what may I have for my tea?"

Then said Nqong from his bath in the salt-pan, "Come and ask me about it to-morrow, because I 'm going to wash."

So they were left in the middle of Australia, Old Man Kangaroo and Yellow-Dog Dingo, and each said, "That 's *your* fault."

This is the mouth-filling song
Of the race that was run by a Boomer,
Run in a single burst—only event of its kind—
Started by Big God Nqong from Warrigaborrigarooma,
Old Man Kangaroo first: Yellow-Dog Dingo behind.

Kangaroo bounded away,
His back-legs working like pistons—
Bounded from morning till dark,
Twenty-five feet to a bound.
Yellow-Dog Dingo lay
Like a yellow cloud in the distance—
Much too busy to bark.
My! but they covered the ground!

Nobody knows where they went,
Or followed the track that they flew in,
For that Continent
Had n't been given a name.
They ran thirty degrees,
From Torres Straits to the Leeuwin
(Look at the Atlas, please),
And they ran back as they came.

S'posing you could trot
From Adelaide to the Pacific,
For an afternoon's run—
Half what these gentlemen did—
You would feel rather hot
But your legs would develop terrific—
Yes, my importunate son,
You 'd be a Marvellous Kid!

VII

FIFTY NORTH AND FORTY WEST

From *Just So Stories*

WHEN the cabin port-holes are dark and green
    Because of the seas outside;
When the ship goes *wop* (with a wiggle between)
And the steward falls into the soup-tureen,
    And the trunks begin to slide;
When Nursey lies on the floor in a heap,
And Mummy tells you to let her sleep,
And you are n't waked or washed or dressed,
Why, then you will know (if you have n't guessed)
You 're "Fifty North and Forty West!"

VIII

TRUE ROYALTY

From *Just So Stories*

For Eleanor who feeds her butterfly on a fresh
red rose "to see him uncoil his proboscis and eat
like a little elephant."

THERE was never a Queen like Balkis,
    From here to the wide world's end;
But Balkis talked to a butterfly
    As you would talk to a friend.

There was never a King like Solomon,
    Not since the world began;
But Solomon talked to a butterfly
    As a man would talk to a man.

She was Queen of Sabæa—
    And *he* was Asia's Lord—
But they both of 'em talked to butterflies
    When they took their walks abroad!

IX

ROLL DOWN TO RIO

From *Just So Stories*

I'VE never sailed the Amazon,
    I've never reached Brazil;
But the *Don* and *Magdalena*,
    They can go there when they will!

        Yes, weekly from Southampton,
        Great steamers, white and gold,
        Go rolling down to Rio
            (Roll down—roll down to Rio!)
        And I'd like to roll to Rio
        Some day before I'm old!

I've never seen a Jaguar,
    Nor yet an Armadill—
O dilloing in his armour,
    And I s'pose I never will,

Unless I go to Rio
These wonders to behold—
Roll down—roll down to Rio—
Roll *really* down to Rio!
Oh, I'd love to roll to Rio
Some day before I'm old!

*"Oh, I'd love to roll to Rio
Some day before I'm old."*

X

THERE RUNS A ROAD BY MERROW DOWN

From Just So Stories

THERE runs a road by Merrow Down—
    A grassy track to-day it is—
An hour out of Guildford town,
    Above the river Wey it is.

Here, when they heard the horse-bells ring
    The ancient Britons dressed and rode
To watch the dark Phœnicians bring
    Their goods along the Western Road.

And here, or hereabouts, they met
    To hold their racial talks and such—
To barter beads for Whitby jet,
    And tin for gay shell torques and such.

But long and long before that time
    (When bison used to roam on it)
Did Taffy and her Daddy climb
    That down, and had their home on it.

Then beavers built in Broadstonebrook
   And made a swamp where Bramley stands;
And bears from Shere would come and look
   For Taffimai where Shamley stands.

The Wey, that Taffy called Wagai,
   Was more than six times bigger then:
And all the Tribe of Tegumai
   They cut a noble figure then!

Of all the Tribe of Tegumai
   Who cut that figure, none remain,—
On Merrow Down the cuckoos cry—
   The silence and the sun remain.

But as the faithful years return
   And hearts unwounded sing again,
Comes Taffy dancing through the fern
   To lead the Surrey spring again.

Her brows are bound with bracken-fronds,
   And golden elf-locks fly above;
Her eyes are bright as diamonds
   And bluer than the skies above.

In mocassins and deer-skin cloak,
   Unfearing, free and fair she flits,
And lights her little damp-wood smoke
   To show her daddy where she flits.

For far—oh, very far behind,
   So far she cannot call to him,
Comes Tegumai alone to find
   The daughter that was all to him.

XI

I KEEP SIX HONEST SERVING–MEN

From *Just So Stories*

I KEEP six honest serving-men;
    (They taught me all I know)
Their names are What and Where and When
    And How and Why and Who.
I send them over land and sea,
    I send them east and west;
But after they have worked for me,
    I give them all a rest.

I let them rest from nine till five,
    For I am busy then,
As well as breakfast, lunch, and tea,
    For they are hungry men:
But different folk have different views;
    I know a person small—
She keeps ten million serving-men,
    Who get no rest at all!

She sends 'em abroad on her own affairs,
    From the second she opens her eyes—
One million Hows, two million Wheres,
    And seven million Whys!

XII

PUSSY AND BINKIE

From *The Just So Song Book*

Pussy can sit by the fire and sing,
    Pussy can climb a tree,
Or play with a silly old cork and string
    To 'muse herself, not me.
But I like *Binkie*, my dog, because
    He knows how to behave;
So, *Binkie's* the same as the First Friend was
    And I am the Man in the Cave.

Pussy will play man-Friday till
    It 's time to wet her paw
And make her walk on the window-sill
    (For the footprint Crusoe saw);
Then she fluffles her tail and mews,
    And scratches and won't attend.
But *Binkie* will play whatever I choose,
    And he is my true First Friend.

Pussy will rub my knees with her head
    Pretending she loves me hard;
But the very minute I go to my bed
    Pussy runs out in the yard,

And there she stays till the morning-light;
    So I know it is only pretend;
But *Binkie,* he snores at my feet all night,
    And he is my Firstest Friend!

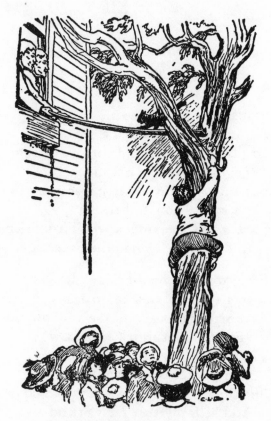

Pussy can climb a tree,
But she cannot always get down.

XIII

WEE WILLIE WINKIE

From *Under the Deodars*

"An officer and a gentleman."

HIS full name was Percival William Williams, but he picked up the other name in a nursery-book, and that was the end of the christened titles. His mother's ayah called him Willie-Baba, but as he never paid the faintest attention to anything that the ayah said, her wisdom did not help matters.

His father was the Colonel of the 195th, and as soon as Wee Willie Winkie was old enough to understand what Military Discipline meant, Colonel Williams put him under it. There was no other way of managing the child. When he was good for a week, he drew good-conduct pay; and when he was bad, he was deprived of his good-conduct stripe. Generally he was bad, for India offers so many chances to little six-year-olds of going wrong.

Children resent familiarity from strangers, and Wee Willie Winkie was a very particular child. Once he accepted an acquaintance, he was graciously pleased to thaw. He accepted

Brandis, a subaltern of the 195th, on sight. Brandis was having tea at the Colonel's, and Wee Willie Winkie entered, strong in the possession of a good-conduct badge won for not chasing the hens round the compound. He regarded Brandis with gravity for at least ten minutes, and then delivered himself of his opinion.

"I like you," said he slowly, getting off his chair and coming over to Brandis. "I like you. I shall call you Coppy, because of your hair. Do you mind being called Coppy? It is because of ve hair, you know."

Here was one of the most embarrassing of Wee Willie Winkie's peculiarities. He would look at a stranger for some time, and then, without warning or explanation, would give him a name. And the name stuck. No regimental penalties could break Wee Willie Winkie of this habit. He lost his good-conduct badge for christening the Commissioner's wife "Pobs"; but nothing that the Colonel could do made the Station forego the nickname, and Mrs. Collen remained Mrs. "Pobs" till the end of her stay. So Brandis was christened "Coppy," and rose, therefore, in the estimation of the regiment.

If Wee Willie Winkie took an interest in anyone, the fortunate man was envied alike by the mess and the rank and file. And in their envy lay no suspicion of self-interest. "The Colonel's son" was idolized on his own merits entirely. Yet Wee Willie Winkie was not lovely. His face was permanently freckled, as his legs were permanently scratched, and in spite of his mother's almost tearful remonstrances he had insisted upon having his long yellow locks cut short in the military fashion. "I want my hair like Sergeant Tummil's," said Wee Willie Winkie, and, his father abetting, the sacrifice was accomplished.

Three weeks after the bestowal of his youthful affections

on Lieutenant Brandis—henceforward to be called "Coppy"
for the sake of brevity—Wee Willie Winkie was destined to
behold strange things and far beyond his comprehension.

Coppy returned his liking with interest. Coppy had let
him wear for five rapturous minutes his own big sword—
just as tall as Wee Willie Winkie. Coppy had promised him
a terrier puppy; and Coppy had permitted him to witness
the miraculous operation of shaving. Nay, more—Coppy
had said that even he, Wee Willie Winkie, would rise in time
to the ownership of a box of shiny knives, a silver soap-box
and a silver-handled "sputter-brush," as Wee Willie Winkie
called it. Decidedly, there was no one, except his father, who
could give or take away good-conduct badges at pleasure,
half so wise, strong, and valiant as Coppy with the Afghan
and Egyptian medals on his breast. Why, then, should Coppy
be guilty of the unmanly weakness of kissing—vehemently
kissing—a "big girl," Miss Allardyce to wit? In the course of
a morning ride, Wee Willie Winkie had seen Coppy so doing, and, like the gentleman he was, had promptly wheeled
round and cantered back to his groom, lest the groom should
also see.

Under ordinary circumstances he would have spoken to
his father, but he felt instinctively that this was a matter on
which Coppy ought first to be consulted.

"Coppy," shouted Wee Willie Winkie, reining up outside
that subaltern's bungalow early one morning—"I want to
see you, Coppy!"

"Come in, young 'un," returned Coppy, who was at early
breakfast in the midst of his dogs. "What mischief have you
been getting into now?"

Wee Willie Winkie had done nothing notoriously bad for
three days, and so stood on a pinnacle of virtue.

"I 've been doing nothing bad," said he, curling himself

into a long chair with a studious affectation of the Colonel's languor after a hot parade. He buried his freckled nose in a tea-cup and, with eyes staring roundly over the rim, asked: "I say, Coppy, is it pwoper to kiss big girls?"

"By Jove! You 're beginning early. Who do you want to kiss?"

"No one. My muvver's always kissing me if I don't stop her. If it is n't pwoper, how was you kissing Major Allardyce's big girl last morning, by ve canal?"

Coppy's brow wrinkled. He and Miss Allardyce had with great craft managed to keep their engagement secret for a fortnight. There were urgent and imperative reasons why Major Allardyce should not know how matters stood for at least another month, and this small marplot had discovered a great deal too much.

"I saw you," said Wee Willie Winkie calmly. "But ve groom did n't see. I said, 'Hut jao.' "

"Oh, you had that much sense, you young Rip," groaned poor Coppy, half amused and half angry. "And how many people may you have told about it?"

"Only me myself. You did n't tell when I twied to wide ve buffalo ven my pony was lame; and I fought you would n't like."

"Winkie," said Coppy enthusiastically, shaking the small hand, "you 're the best of good fellows. Look here, you can't understand all these things. One of these days—hang it, how can I make you see it!—I 'm going to marry Miss Allardyce, and then she 'll be Mrs. Coppy, as you say. If your young mind is so scandalized at the idea of kissing big girls, go and tell your father."

"What will happen?" said Wee Willie Winkie, who firmly believed that his father was omnipotent.

"I shall get into trouble," said Coppy, playing his trump card with an appealing look at the holder of the ace.

"Ven I won't," said Wee Willie Winkie briefly. "But my faver says it 's un-man-ly to be always kissing, and I did n't fink you 'd do vat, Coppy."

"I 'm not always kissing, old chap. It 's only now and then, and when you 're bigger you 'll do it too. Your father meant it 's not good for little boys."

"Ah!" said Wee Willie Winkie, now fully enlightened. "It 's like ve sputter-brush?"

"Exactly," said Coppy gravely.

"But I don't fink I 'll ever want to kiss big girls, nor no one, 'cept my muvver. And I must vat, you know."

There was a long pause, broken by Wee Willie Winkie.

"Are you fond of vis big girl, Coppy?"

"Awfully!" said Coppy.

"Fonder van you are of Bell or ve Butcha—or me?"

"It 's in a different way," said Coppy. "You see, one of these days Miss Allardyce will belong to me, but you 'll grow up and command the Regiment and—all sorts of things. It 's quite different, you see."

"Very well," said Wee Willie Winkie, rising. "If you 're fond of ve big girl, I won't tell anyone. I must go now."

Coppy rose and escorted his small guest to the door, adding: "You 're the best of little fellows, Winkie. I tell you what. In thirty days from now you can tell if you like—tell anyone you like."

Thus the secret of the Brandis-Allardyce engagement was dependent on a little child's word. Coppy, who knew Wee Willie Winkie's idea of truth, was at ease, for he felt that he would not break promises. Wee Willie Winkie betrayed a special and unusual interest in Miss Allardyce, and, slowly revolving round that embarrassed young lady, was used to regard her gravely with unwinking eye. He was trying to discover why Coppy should have kissed her. She was not half so nice as his own mother. On the other hand she was Coppy's property, and would in time belong to him. Therefore it behooved him to treat her with as much respect as Coppy's big sword or shiny pistol.

The idea that he shared a great secret in common with Coppy kept Wee Willie Winkie unusually virtuous for three weeks. Then the Old Adam broke out, and he made what he called a "camp-fire" at the bottom of the garden. How could he have foreseen that the flying sparks would have lighted the Colonel's little hay-rick and consumed a week's store for the horses? Sudden and swift was the punishment—deprivation of the good-conduct badge and, most sorrowful of all, two days' confinement to barracks—the house and veranda—coupled with the withdrawal of the light of his father's countenance.

He took the sentence like the man he strove to be, drew himself up with a quivering under-lip, saluted, and, once clear of the room, ran to weep bitterly in his nursery—called by him "my quarters." Coppy came in the afternoon and attempted to console the culprit.

"I'm under awwest," said Wee Willie Winkie mournfully, "and I did n't ought to speak to you."

Very early the next morning he climbed on to the roof of the house—that was not forbidden—and beheld Miss Allardyce going for a ride.

"Where are you going?" cried Wee Willie Winkie.

"Across the river," she answered, and trotted forward.

Now the cantonment in which the 195th lay was bounded on the north by a river—dry in the winter. From his earliest years, Wee Willie Winkie had been forbidden to go across the river, and had noted that even Coppy—the almost almighty Coppy—had never set foot beyond it. Wee Willie Winkie had once been read to, out of a big blue book, the history of the Princess and the Goblins—a most wonderful tale of a land where the Goblins were always warring with the children of men until they were defeated by one Curdie. Ever since that date it seemed to him that the bare black and purple hills across the river were inhabited by Goblins, and, in truth, everyone had said that there lived the Bad Men. Even in his own house the lower halves of the windows were covered with green paper on account of the Bad Men who might, if allowed clear view, fire into peaceful drawing-rooms and comfortable bedrooms. Certainly, beyond the river, which was the end of all the Earth, lived the Bad Men. And here was Major Allardyce's big girl, Coppy's property, preparing to venture into their borders! What would Coppy say if anything happened to her? If the Goblins ran off with her as they did with Curdie's Princess? She must at all hazards be turned back.

The house was still. Wee Willie Winkie reflected for a moment on the very terrible wrath of his father; and then—broke his arrest! It was a crime unspeakable. The low sun threw his shadow, very large and very black, on the trim garden-paths, as he went down to the stables and ordered his pony. It seemed to him in the hush of the dawn that all the big world had been bidden to stand still and look at Wee Willie Winkie guilty of mutiny. The drowsy groom handed him his mount, and since the one great sin made all others insignificant, Wee Willie Winkie said that he was going to ride over to Coppy Sahib, and went out at a foot-pace, stepping on the soft mould of the flower-borders.

The devastating track of the pony's feet was the last misdeed that cut him off from all sympathy of Humanity. He turned into the road, leaned forward, and rode as fast as the pony could put foot to the ground in the direction of the river.

But the liveliest of twelve-two ponies can do little against the long canter of a Waler. Miss Allardyce was far ahead, had passed through the crops, beyond the Police-post, when all the guards were asleep, and her mount was scattering the pebbles of the river bed as Wee Willie Winkie left the cantonment and British India behind him. Bowed, forward and still flogging, Wee Willie Winkie shot into Afghan terri-tory, and could just see Miss Allardyce a black speck, flicker-ing across the stony plain. The reason of her wandering was simple enough. Coppy, in a tone of too-hastily-assumed authority, had told her over night that she must not ride out by the river. And she had gone to prove her own spirit and teach Coppy a lesson.

Almost at the foot of the inhospitable hills Wee Willie Winkie saw the Waler blunder and come down heavily. Miss Allardyce struggled clear, but her ankle had been severely twisted, and she could not stand. Having thus demonstrated her spirit, she wept copiously, and was surprised by the apparition of a white, wide-eyed child in khaki, on a nearly spent pony.

"Are you badly, badly hurted?" shouted Wee Willie Winkie, as soon as he was within range. "You did n't ought to be here."

"I don't know," said Miss Allardyce ruefully, ignoring the reproof. "Good gracious, child, what are you doing here?"

"You said you was going acwoss ve wiver," panted Wee Willie Winkie, throwing himself off his pony. "And nobody —not even Coppy—must go acwoss ve wiver, and I came after you ever so hard, but you would n't stop, and now you 've hurted yourself, and Coppy will be angry wiv me, and—I 've bwoken my awwest! I 've bwoken my awwest!"

The future Colonel of the 195th sat down and sobbed. In spite of the pain in her ankle the girl was moved.

"Have you ridden all the way from cantonments, little man? What for?"

"You belonged to Coppy. Coppy told me so!" wailed Wee Willie Winkie disconsolately. "I saw him kissing you, and he said he was fonder of you van Bell or ve Butcha or me. And so I came. You must get up and come back. You did n't ought to be here. Vis is a bad place, and I 've bwoken my awwest."

"I can't move, Winkie," said Miss Allardyce, with a groan. "I 've hurt my foot. What shall I do?"

She showed a readiness to weep afresh which steadied Wee Willie Winkie, who had been brought up to believe that tears were the depth of unmanliness. Still, when one is as great a sinner as Wee Willie Winkie, even a man may be permitted to break down.

"Winkie," said Miss Allardyce, "when you 've rested a little, ride back and tell them to send out something to carry me back in. It hurts fearfully."

The child sat still for a little time and Miss Allardyce closed her eyes; the pain was nearly making her faint. She was roused by Wee Willie Winkie tying up the reins on his pony's neck and setting it free with a vicious cut of his whip that made it whicker. The little animal headed toward the cantonments.

"Oh, Winkie! What are you doing?"

"Hush!" said Wee Willie Winkie. "Vere 's a man coming— one of ve Bad Men. I must stay wiv you. My faver says a man must always look after a girl. Jack will go home, and ven vey 'll come and look for us. Vat 's why I let him go."

Not one man, but two or three, had appeared from behind the rocks of the hills, and the heart of Wee Willie Winkie sank within him, for just in this manner were the Goblins wont to steal out and vex Curdie's soul. Thus had they played in Curdie's garden, he had seen the picture, and thus had they frightened the Princess's nurse. He heard them talking to each other, and recognized with joy the bastard Pushto that he had picked up from one of his father's grooms lately dismissed. People who spoke that tongue could not be the Bad Men. They were only natives, after all.

They came up to the boulders on which Miss Allardyce's horse had blundered.

Then rose from the rock Wee Willie Winkie, child of the Dominant Race, aged six and three-quarters, and said briefly and emphatically "Jao!" The pony had crossed the river-bed.

The men laughed, and laughter from natives was the one thing Wee Willie Winkie could not tolerate. He asked them what they wanted and why they did not depart. Other men with most evil faces and crooked-stocked guns crept out of the shadows of the hills, till, soon, Wee Willie Winkie was face to face with an audience some twenty strong. Miss Allardyce screamed.

"Who are you?" said one of the men.

"I am the Colonel Sahib's son, and my order is that you go at once. You black men are frightening the Miss Sahib. One of you must run into cantonments and take the news that the Miss Sahib has hurt herself, and that the Colonel's son is here with her."

"Put our feet into the trap?" was the laughing reply. "Hear this boy's speech!"

"Say that I sent you—I, the Colonel's son. They will give you money."

"What is the use of this talk? Take up the child and the

girl, and we can at least ask for the ransom. Ours are the villages on the heights," said a voice in the background.

These were the Bad Men—worse than Goblins—and it needed all Wee Willie Winkie's training to prevent him from bursting into tears. But he felt that to cry before a native, excepting only his mother's ayah, would be an infamy greater than any mutiny. Moreover, he, as future Colonel of the 195th, had that grim regiment at his back.

"Are you going to carry us away?" said Wee Willie Winkie, very blanched and uncomfortable.

"Yes, my little Sahib Bahadur," said the tallest of the men, "and eat you afterward."

"That is child's talk," said Wee Willie Winkie. "Men do not eat men."

A yell of laughter interrupted him, but he went on firmly —"And if you do carry us away, I tell you that all my regiment will come up in a day and kill you all without leaving one. Who will take my message to the Colonel Sahib?"

Speech in any vernacular—and Wee Willie Winkie had a colloquial acquaintance with three—was easy to the boy who could not yet manage his "r's" and "th's" aright.

Another man joined the conference, crying: "Oh, foolish men! What this babe says is true. He is the heart's heart of those white troops. For the sake of peace let them go both, for if he be taken, the regiment will break loose and gut the valley. Our villages are in the valley, and we shall not escape. That regiment are devils. They broke Khoda Yar's breast-bone with kicks when he tried to take the rifles; and if we touch this child they will fire and rape and plunder for a month, till nothing remains. Better to send a man back to take the message and get a reward. I say that this child is their God, and that they will spare none of us, nor our women, if we harm him."

It was Din Mahommed, the dismissed groom of the Colonel, who made the diversion, and an angry and heated discussion followed. Wee Willie Winkie, standing over Miss Allardyce, waited the upshot. Surely his "wegiment," his own "wegiment," would not desert him if they knew of his extremity.

The riderless pony brought the news to the 195th, though there had been consternation in the Colonel's household for an hour before. The little beast came in through the parade-ground in front of the main barracks, where the men were settling down to play Spoil-five till the afternoon. Devlin, the Colour Sergeant of E Company, glanced at the empty saddle and tumbled through the barrack-rooms, kicking up each Room Corporal as he passed. "Up, ye beggars! There 's something happened to the Colonel's son," he shouted.

"He could n't fall off! S 'elp me, 'e could n't fall off," blubbered a drummer-boy. "Go an' hunt acrost the river. He 's over there if he 's anywhere, an' maybe those Pathans have got 'im. For the love o' Gawd don't look for 'im in the nullahs! Let 's go over the river."

"There 's sense in Mott yet," said Devlin. "E Company, double out to the river—sharp!"

So E Company, in its shirt-sleeves mainly, doubled for the dear life, and in the rear toiled the perspiring Sergeant, adjuring it to double yet faster. The cantonment was alive with the men of the 195th hunting for Wee Willie Winkie, and the Colonel finally overtook E Company, far too exhausted to swear, struggling in the pebbles of the river-bed.

Up the hill under which Wee Willie Winkie's Bad Men were discussing the wisdom of carrying off the child and the girl, a lookout fired two shots.

"What have I said?" shouted Din Mahommed. "There is

the warning! The pulton are out already and are coming across the plain! Get away! Let us not be seen with the boy!"

The men waited for an instant, and then, as another shot was fired, withdrew into the hills, silently as they had appeared.

"The wegiment is coming," said Wee Willie Winkie confidently to Miss Allardyce, "and it's all wight. Don't cwy!"

He needed the advice himself, for ten minutes later, when his father came up, he was weeping bitterly with his head in Miss Allardyce's lap.

And the men of the 195th carried him home with shouts and rejoicings; and Coppy, who had ridden a horse into a lather, met him, and, to his intense disgust, kissed him openly in the presence of the men.

But there was balm for his dignity. His father assured him that not only would the breaking of arrest be condoned, but that the good-conduct badge would be restored as soon as his mother could sew it on his blouse-sleeve. Miss Allardyce had told the Colonel a story that made him proud of his son.

"She belonged to you, Coppy," said Wee Willie Winkie, indicating Miss Allardyce with a grimy forefinger. "I knew she did n't ought to go acwoss ve wiver, and I knew ve wegiment would come to me if I sent Jack home."

"You 're a hero, Winkie," said Coppy—"a pukka hero!"

"I don't know what vat means," said Wee Willie Winkie, "but you must n't call me Winkie any no more. I 'm Percival Will'am Will'ams."

And in this manner did Wee Willie Winkie enter into his manhood.

XIV

BAA, BAA, BLACK SHEEP

From *Under the Deodars*

Baa, Baa, Black Sheep,
Have you any wool?
Yes, Sir; yes, Sir; three bags full.
One for the Master, one for the Dame—
None for the Little Boy that cries down the lane.
                    —NURSERY RHYME.

THE FIRST BAG

"When I was in my father's house, I was in a better place."

THEY were putting Punch to bed—the ayah and the hamal, and Meeta, the big Surti boy with the red and gold turban. Judy, already tucked inside her mosquito-curtains, was nearly asleep. Punch had been allowed to stay up for dinner. Many privileges had been accorded to Punch within the last ten days, and a greater kindness from the people of his world had encompassed his ways and works, which were mostly obstreperous. He sat on the edge of his bed and swung his bare legs defiantly.

"Punch-baba going to bye-lo?" said the ayah suggestively.

"No," said Punch. "Punch-baba wants the story about

the Ranee that was turned into a tiger. Meeta must tell it, and the hamal shall hide behind the door and make tiger-noises at the proper time."

"But Judy-baba will wake up," said the ayah.

"Judy-baba is waking," piped a small voice from the mosquito-curtains. "There was a Ranee that lived at Delhi. Go on, Meeta," and she fell asleep again while Meeta began the story.

Never had Punch secured the telling of that tale with so little opposition. He reflected for a long time. The hamal made the tiger-noises in twenty different keys.

" 'Top!" said Punch authoritatively. "Why does n't Papa come in and say he is going to give me put-put?"

"Punch-baba is going away," said the ayah. "In another week there will be no Punch-baba to pull my hair any more." She sighed softly, for the boy of the household was very dear to her heart.

"Up the Ghauts in a train?" said Punch, standing on his bed. "All the way to Nassick, where the Ranee-Tiger lives?"

"Not to Nassick this year, little Sahib," said Meeta, lifting him on his shoulder. "Down to the sea where the cocoanuts are thrown, and across the sea in a big ship. Will you take Meeta with you to Belait?"

"You shall all come," said Punch, from the height of Meeta's strong arms. "Meeta and the ayah and the hamal and Bhini-in-the-Garden, and the salaam-Captain-Sahib-snake-man."

There was no mockery in Meeta's voice when he replied—"Great is the Sahib's favour," and laid the little man down in the bed, while the ayah, sitting in the moonlight at the doorway, lulled him to sleep with an interminable canticle such as they sing in the Roman Catholic Church at Parel. Punch curled himself into a ball and slept.

Next morning Judy shouted that there was a rat in the nursery, and thus he forgot to tell her the wonderful news. It did not much matter, for Judy was only three and she would not have understood. But Punch was five; and he knew that going to England would be much nicer than a trip to Nassick.

And Papa and Mamma sold the brougham and the piano, and stripped the house, and curtailed the allowance of crockery for the daily meals, and took long council together over a bundle of letters bearing the Rocklington postmark.

"The worst of it is that one can't be certain of anything," said Papa, pulling his moustache. "The letters in themselves are excellent, and the terms are moderate enough."

"The worst of it is that the children will grow up away from me," thought Mamma; but she did not say it aloud.

"We are only one case among hundreds," said Papa bitterly. "You shall go Home again in five years, dear."

"Punch will be ten then—and Judy eight. Oh, how long and long and long the time will be! And we have to leave them among strangers."

"Punch is a cheery little chap. He's sure to make friends wherever he goes."

"And who could help loving my Ju?"

They were standing over the cots in the nursery late at night, and I think that Mamma was crying softly. After Papa had gone away, she knelt down by the side of Judy's cot. The ayah saw her and put up a prayer that the memsahib might never find the love of her children taken away from her and given to a stranger.

Mamma's own prayer was a slightly illogical one. Summarized it ran: "Let strangers love my children and be as good to them as I should be, but let me preserve their love

and their confidence for ever and ever. Amen." Punch
scratched himself in his sleep, and Judy moaned a little. That
seems to be the only answer to the prayer: and, next day,
they all went down to the sea, and there was a scene at the
Apollo Bunder when Punch discovered that Meeta could not
come too, and Judy learned that the ayah must be left behind. But Punch found a thousand fascinating things in the
rope, block, and steam-pipe line on the big P. and O.
Steamer, long before Meeta and the ayah had dried their
tears.

"Come back, Punch-baba," said the ayah.

"Come back," said Meeta, "and be a Burra Sahib."

"Yes," said Punch, lifted up in his father's arms to wave
good-bye. "Yes, I will come back, and I will be a Burra
Sahib Bahadur!"

At the end of the first day Punch demanded to be set
down in England, which he was certain must be close at
hand. Next day there was a merry breeze, and Punch was
very sick. "When I come back to Bombay," said Punch on
his recovery, "I will come by the road—in a broom-gharri.
This is a very naughty ship."

The Swedish boatswain consoled him, and he modified his
opinions as the voyage went on. There was so much to see
and to handle and ask questions about that Punch nearly
forgot the ayah and Meeta and the hamal, and with difficulty
remembered a few words of the Hindustani once his second-
speech.

But Judy was much worse. The day before the steamer
reached Southampton, Mamma asked her if she would not
like to see the ayah again. Judy's blue eyes turned to the
stretch of sea that had swallowed all her tiny past, and she
said: "Ayah! What ayah?"

Mamma cried over her, and Punch marveled. It was then

that he heard for the first time Mamma's passionate appeal to him never to let Judy forget Mamma. Seeing that Judy was young, ridiculously young, and that Mamma, every evening for four weeks past, had come into the cabin to sing her and Punch to sleep with a mysterious tune that he called "Sonny, my soul," Punch could not understand what Mamma meant. But he strove to do his duty, for the moment Mamma left the cabin, he said to Judy: "Ju, you bemember Mamma?"

" 'Torse I do," said Judy.

"Then always bemember Mamma, 'r else I won't give you the paper ducks that the red-haired Captain Sahib cut out for me."

So Judy promised always to "bemember Mamma."

Many and many a time was Mamma's command laid upon Punch, and Papa would say the same thing with an insistence that awed the child.

"You must make haste and learn to write, Punch," said Papa, "and then you 'll be able to write letters to us in Bombay."

"I 'll come into your room," said Punch, and Papa choked.

Papa and Mamma were always choking in those days. If Punch took Judy to task for not "bemembering," they choked. If Punch sprawled on the sofa in the Southampton lodging-house and sketched his future in purple and gold, they choked; and so they did if Judy put up her mouth for a kiss.

Through many days all four were vagabonds on the face of the earth: Punch with no one to give orders to, Judy too young for anything, and Papa and Mamma grave, distracted, and choking.

"Where," demanded Punch, wearied of a loathsome contrivance on four wheels with a mound of luggage atop—

"where is our broom-gharri? This thing talks so much that I can't talk. Where is our own broom-gharri? When I was at Bandstand before we comed away, I asked Inverarity Sahib why he was sitting in it, and he said it was his own. And I said, 'I will give it you'—I like Inverarity Sahib—and I said, 'Can you put your legs through the pully-wag loops by the windows?' And Inverarity Sahib said 'No,' and laughed. I can put my legs through the pully-wag loops. I can put my legs through these pully-wag loops. Look! Oh, Mamma 's crying again! I did n't know. I was n't not to do so."

Punch drew his legs out of the loops of the four-wheeler: the door opened and he slid to the earth, in a cascade of parcels, at the door of an austere little villa whose gates bore the legend "Downe Lodge." Punch gathered himself together and eyed the house with disfavour. It stood on a sandy road, and a cold wind tickled his knickerbockered legs.

"Let us go away," said Punch. "This is not a pretty place."

But Mamma and Papa and Judy had quitted the cab, and all the luggage was being taken into the house. At the doorstep stood a woman in black, and she smiled largely, with dry chapped lips. Behind her was a man, big, bony, gray, and lame as to one leg—behind him a boy of twelve, black-haired and oily in appearance. Punch surveyed the trio, and advanced without fear, as he had been accustomed to do in Bombay when callers came and he happened to be playing in the veranda.

"How do you do?" said he. "I am Punch." But they were all looking at the luggage—all except the gray man, who shook hands with Punch and said he was a "smart little fellow." There was much running about and banging of boxes, and Punch curled himself up on the sofa in the dining-room and considered things.

"I don't like these people," said Punch. "But never mind.

We 'll go away soon. We have always went away soon from everywhere. I wish we was gone back to Bombay soon."

The wish bore no fruit. For six days Mamma wept at intervals, and showed the woman in black all Punch's clothes —a liberty which Punch resented. "But p'raps she 's a new white ayah," he thought. "I 'm to call her Antirosa, but she does n't call me Sahib. She says just Punch," he confided to Judy. "What is Antirosa?"

Judy did n't know. Neither she nor Punch had heard anything of an animal called an aunt. Their world had been Papa and Mamma, who knew everything, permitted everything, and loved everybody—even Punch when he used to go into the garden at Bombay and fill his nails with mold after the weekly nail-cutting, because, as he explained between two strokes of the slipper to his sorely tried Father, his fingers "felt so new at the ends."

In an undefined way Punch judged it advisable to keep both parents between himself and the woman in black and the boy in black hair. He did not approve of them. He liked the gray man, who had expressed a wish to be called "Uncle-harri." They nodded at each other when they met, and the gray man showed him a little ship with rigging that took up and down.

"She is a model of the *Brisk*—the little *Brisk* that was sore exposed that day at Navarino." The gray man hummed the last words and fell into a reverie. "I 'll tell you about Navarino, Punch, when we go for walks together; and you must n't touch the ship, because she 's the *Brisk*."

Long before that walk, the first of many, was taken, they roused Punch and Judy in the chill dawn of a February morning to say Good-bye; and of all people in the wide earth to Papa and Mamma—both crying this time. Punch was very sleepy and Judy was cross.

"Don't forget us," pleaded Mamma. "Oh, my little son, don't forget us, and see that Judy remembers too."

"I 've told Judy to bemember," said Punch, wiggling, for his father's beard tickled his neck. "I 've told Judy—ten—forty—'leven thousand times. But Ju 's so young—quite a baby—is n't she?"

"Yes," said Papa, "quite a baby, and you must be good to Judy, and make haste to learn to write and—and—and——"

Punch was back in his bed again. Judy was fast asleep, and there was the rattle of a cab below. Papa and Mamma had gone away. Not to Nassick; that was across the sea. To some place much nearer, of course, and equally of course they would return. They came back after dinner-parties, and Papa had come back after he had been to a place called "The Snows," and Mamma with him, to Punch and Judy at Mrs. Inverarity's house in Marine Lines. Assuredly they would come back again. So Punch fell asleep till the true morning, when the black-haired boy met him with the information that Papa and Mamma had gone to Bombay, and that he and Judy were to stay at Downe Lodge "forever." Antirosa, tearfully appealed to for a contradiction, said that Harry had spoken the truth, and that it behooved Punch to fold up his clothes neatly on going to bed. Punch went out and wept bitterly with Judy, into whose fair head he had driven some ideas of the meaning of separation.

When a matured man discovers that he has been deserted by Providence, deprived of his God, and cast without help, comfort, or sympathy, upon a world which is new and strange to him, his despair, which may find expression in evil-living, the writing of his experiences, or the more satisfactory diversion of suicide, is generally supposed to be impressive. A child, under exactly similar circumstances as far as its knowledge goes, cannot very well curse God and die. It howls till its nose is red, its eyes are sore, and its head aches. Punch and Judy, through no fault of their own, had lost all their world. They sat in the hall and cried; the black-haired boy looking on from afar.

The model of the ship availed nothing, though the gray man assured Punch that he might pull the rigging up and down as much as he pleased; and Judy was promised free entry into the kitchen. They wanted Papa and Mamma, gone to Bombay beyond the seas, and their grief while it lasted was without remedy.

When the tears ceased the house was very still. Antirosa had decided it was better to let the children "have their cry out," and the boy had gone to school. Punch raised his head from the floor and sniffed mournfully. Judy was nearly asleep. Three short years had not taught her how to bear sorrow with full knowledge. There was a distant, dull boom in the air—a repeated heavy thud. Punch knew that sound in Bombay in the Monsoon. It was the sea—the sea that must be traversed before anyone could get to Bombay.

"Quick, Ju!" he cried, "we 're close to the sea. I can hear it! Listen! That 's where they 've went. P'raps we can catch them if we was in time. They did n't mean to go without us. They 've only forgot."

"Iss," said Judy. "They 've only forgotted. Less go to the sea."

The hall-door was open and so was the garden-gate.

"It 's very, very big, this place," he said, looking cautiously down the road, "and we will get lost; but I will find a man and order him to take me back to my house—like I did in Bombay."

He took Judy by the hand, and the two fled hatless in the direction of the sound of the sea. Downe Villa was almost the last of a range of newly built houses running out, through a

chaos of brick-mounds, to a heath where gypsies occasion-
ally camped and where the Garrison Artillery of Rocklington practised. There were few people to be seen, and the
children might have been taken for those of the soldiery, who
ranged far. Half an hour the wearied little legs tramped
across heath, potato-field, and sand-dune.

"I 'se so tired," said Judy, "and Mamma will be angry."

"Mamma 's never angry. I suppose she is waiting at the sea
now while Papa gets tickets. We 'll find them and go along
with them. Ju, you must n't sit down. Only a little more and
we 'll come to the sea. Ju, if you sit down I 'll thmack you!"
said Punch.

They climbed another dune, and came upon the great
gray sea at low tide. Hundreds of crabs were scuttling about
the beach, but there was no trace of Papa and Mamma, not
even of a ship upon the waters—nothing but sand and mud
for miles and miles.

And "Uncleharri" found them by chance—very muddy
and very forlorn—Punch dissolved in tears, but trying to
divert Judy with an "ickle trab," and Judy wailing to
the pitiless horizon for "Mamma, Mamma!"—and again
"Mamma!"

THE SECOND BAG

Ah, well-a-day, for we are souls bereaved!
Of all the creatures under Heaven's wide scope
We are most hopeless, who had once most hope,
And most beliefless, who had most believed.
        —*The City of Dreadful Night.*

All this time not a word about Black Sheep. He came later,
and Harry, the black-haired boy, was mainly responsible for
his coming. Judy—who could help loving little Judy?—
passed, by special permit, into the kitchen and thence

straight to Aunty Rosa's heart. Harry was Aunty Rosa's one child, and Punch was the extra boy about the house. There was no special place for him or his little affairs, and he was forbidden to sprawl on sofas and explain his ideas about the manufacture of this world and his hopes for his future. Sprawling was lazy and wore out sofas, and little boys were not expected to talk. They were talked to, and the talking to was intended for the benefit of their morals. As the un-questioned despot of the house at Bombay, Punch could not quite understand how he came to be of no account in this new life.

Harry might reach across the table and take what he wanted; Judy might point and get what she wanted. Punch was forbidden to do either. The gray man was his great hope and stand-by for many months after Mamma and Papa left, and he had forgotten to tell Judy to "bemember Mamma."

This lapse was excusable, because in the interval he had been introduced by Aunty Rosa to two very impressive things—an abstraction called God, the intimate friend and ally of Aunty Rosa, generally believed to live behind the kitchen-range because it was hot there—and a dirty brown book filled with unintelligible dots and marks. Punch was always anxious to oblige everybody. He, therefore, welded the story of the Creation on to what he could recollect of his Indian fairy tales, and scandalized Aunty Rosa by repeat-ing the result to Judy. It was a sin, a grievous sin, and Punch was talked to for a quarter of an hour. He could not under-stand where the iniquity came in, but was careful not to repeat the offence, because Aunty Rosa told him that God had heard every word he had said and was very angry. If this were true why did n't God come and say so, thought Punch, and dismissed the matter from his mind. Afterward he learned to know the Lord as the only thing in the world more awful than Aunty Rosa—as a Creature that stood in the background and counted the strokes of the cane.

But the reading was, just then, a much more serious matter than any creed. Aunty Rosa sat him upon a table and told him that A B meant ab.

"Why?" said Punch. "A is a and B is bee. Why does A B mean ab?"

"Because I tell you it does," said Aunty Rosa, "and you 've got to say it."

Punch said it accordingly, and for a month, hugely against his will, stumbled through the brown book, not in the least comprehending what it meant. But Uncle Harry, who walked much and generally alone, was wont to come into the nursery and suggest to Aunty Rosa that Punch should walk with him. He seldom spoke, but he showed Punch all Rocklington, from the mud-banks and the sand of the back-bay to the great harbours where ships lay at anchor, and the dockyards where the hammers were never still, and the marine-store shops, and the shiny brass counters in the Offices where Uncle Harry went once every three months with a slip of blue paper and received sovereigns in exchange; for he held a wound-pension. Punch heard, too, from his lips the story of the battle of Navarino, where the sailors of the Fleet, for three days afterward, were deaf as posts and could only sign to each other. "That was because of the noise of the guns," said Uncle Harry, "and I have got the wadding of a bullet somewhere inside me now."

Punch regarded him with curiosity. He had not the least idea what wadding was, and his notion of a bullet was a dockyard cannon-ball bigger than his own head. How could Uncle Harry keep a cannon-ball inside him? He was ashamed to ask, for fear Uncle Harry might be angry.

Punch had never known what anger—real anger—meant

until one terrible day when Harry had taken his paint-box to paint a boat with, and Punch had protested with a loud and lamentable voice. Then Uncle Harry had appeared on the scene and, muttering something about "strangers' children," had with a stick smitten the black-haired boy across the shoulders till he wept and yelled, and Aunty Rosa came in and abused Uncle Harry for cruelty to his own flesh and blood, and Punch shuddered to the tips of his shoes. "It was n't my fault," he explained to the boy, but both Harry and Aunty Rosa said that it was, and that Punch had told tales, and for a week there were no more walks with Uncle Harry.

But that week brought a great joy to Punch.

He had repeated till he was thrice weary the statement that "the Cat lay on the Mat and the Rat came in."

"Now I can truly read," said Punch, "and now I will never read anything in the world."

He put the brown book in the cupboard where his school-books lived and accidentally tumbled out a venerable volume, without covers, labelled *Sharpe's Magazine.* There was the most portentous picture of a Griffin on the first page, with verses below. The Griffin carried off one sheep a day from a German village, till a man came with a "falchion" and split the Griffin open. Goodness only knew what a falchion was, but there was the Griffin, and his history was an improvement upon the eternal Cat.

"This," said Punch, "means things, and now I will know all about everything in all the world." He read till the light failed, not understanding a tithe of the meaning, but tantalized by glimpses of new worlds hereafter to be revealed.

"What is a 'falchion'? What is a 'e-wee lamb'? What is a 'base ussurper'? What is a 'verdant me-ad'? he demanded, with flushed cheeks, at bedtime, of the astonished Aunt Rosa.

"Say your prayers and go to sleep," she replied, and that was all the help Punch then or afterward found at her hands in the new and delightful exercise of reading.

"Aunt Rosa only knows about God and things like that," argued Punch. "Uncle Harry will tell me."

The next walk proved that Uncle Harry could not help either; but he allowed Punch to talk, and even sat down on a bench to hear about the Griffin. Other walks brought other stories as Punch ranged farther afield, for the house held large store of old books that no one ever opened—from Frank Fairlegh in serial numbers, and the earlier poems of Tennyson, contributed anonymously to *Sharpe's Magazine*, to '62 Exhibition Catalogues, gay with colours and delightfully incomprehensible, and odd leaves of "Gulliver's Travels."

As soon as Punch could string a few pot-hooks together, he wrote to Bombay, demanding by return of post "all the books in all the world." Papa could not comply with this modest indent, but sent "Grimm's Fairy Tales" and a "Hans Andersen." That was enough. If he were only left alone Punch could pass, at any hour he chose, into a land of his own, beyond reach of Aunty Rosa and her God, Harry and his teasements, and Judy's claims to be played with.

"Don't disturb me, I'm reading. Go and play in the kitchen," grunted Punch. "Aunty Rosa lets you go there." Judy was cutting her second teeth and was fretful. She appealed to Aunty Rosa, who descended on Punch.

"I was reading," he explained, "reading a book. I want to read."

"You're only doing that to show off," said Aunty Rosa. "But we'll see. Play with Judy now, and don't open a book for a week."

Judy did not pass a very enjoyable playtime with Punch,

who was consumed with indignation. There was a pettiness at the bottom of the prohibition which puzzled him.

"It 's what I like to do," he said, "and she 's found out that and stopped me. Don't cry, Ju—it was n't your fault—please don't cry, or she 'll say I made you."

Ju loyally mopped up her tears, and the two played in their nursery, a room in the basement and half underground, to which they were regularly sent after the midday dinner while Aunty Rosa slept. She drank wine—that is to say, something from a bottle in the cellaret—for her stomach's sake, but if she did not fall asleep she would sometimes come into the nursery to see that the children were really playing. Now bricks, wooden hoops, ninepins, and chinaware cannot amuse forever, especially when all Fairyland is to be won by the mere opening of a book, and, as often as not, Punch would be discovered reading to Judy or telling her interminable tales. That was an offence in the eyes of the law, and Judy would be whisked off by Aunty Rosa, while Punch was left to play alone, "and be sure that I hear you doing it."

It was not a cheering employ, for he had to make a playful noise. At last, with infinite craft, he devised an arrangement whereby the table could be supported as to three legs on toy bricks, leaving the fourth clear to bring down on the floor. He could work the table with one hand and hold a book with the other. This he did till an evil day when Aunty Rosa pounced upon him unawares and told him that he was "acting a lie."

"If you 're old enough to do that," she said—her temper was always worst after dinner—"you 're old enough to be beaten."

"But—I 'm—I 'm not a animal!" said Punch, aghast. He remembered Uncle Harry and the stick, and turned white. Aunty Rosa had hidden a light cane behind her, and Punch was beaten then and there over the shoulders. It was a revelation to him. The room door was shut, and he was left to weep himself into repentance and work out his own Gospel of Life.

Aunty Rosa, he argued, had the power to beat him with many stripes. It was unjust and cruel and Mamma and Papa would never have allowed it. Unless perhaps, as Aunty Rosa seemed to imply, they had sent secret orders. In which case he was abandoned indeed. It would be discreet in the future to propitiate Aunty Rosa, but, then, again, even in matters in which he was innocent, he had been accused of wishing to "show off." He had "shown off" before visitors when he had attacked a strange gentleman—Harry's uncle, not his own—with requests for information about the Griffin and the falchion, and the precise nature of the Tilbury in which Frank Fairlegh rode—all points of paramount interest which he was bursting to understand. Clearly it would not do to pretend to care for Aunty Rosa.

At this point Harry entered and stood afar off, eying Punch, a disheveled heap in the corner of the room, with disgust.

"You're a liar—a young liar," said Harry, with great unction, "and you're to have tea down here because you're not fit to speak to us. And you're not to speak to Judy again till Mother gives you leave. You'll corrupt her. You're only fit to associate with the servant. Mother says so."

Having reduced Punch to a second agony of tears Harry departed up-stairs with the news that Punch was still rebellious.

Uncle Harry sat uneasily in the dining-room. "D—— it all, Rosa," said he at last, "can't you leave the child alone? He's a good enough little chap when I meet him."

"He puts on his best manners with you, Henry," said

Aunty Rosa, "but I'm afraid, I'm very much afraid, that he is the Black Sheep of the family."

Harry heard and stored up the name for future use. Judy cried till she was bidden to stop, her brother not being worth tears; and the evening concluded with the return of Punch to the upper regions and a private sitting at which all the blinding horrors of Hell were revealed to Punch with such store of imagery as Aunty Rosa's narrow mind possessed.

Most grievous of all was Judy's round-eyed reproach, and Punch went to bed in the depths of the Valley of Humiliation. He shared his room with Harry and knew the torture in store. For an hour and a half he had to answer that young gentleman's question as to his motives for telling a lie, and a grievous lie, the precise quantity of punishment inflicted by Aunty Rosa, and had also to profess his deep gratitude for such religious instruction as Harry thought fit to impart.

From that day began the downfall of Punch, now Black Sheep.

"Untrustworthy in one thing, untrustworthy in all," said Aunty Rosa, and Harry felt that Black Sheep was delivered into his hands. He would wake him up in the night to ask him why he was such a liar.

"I don't know," Punch would reply.

"Then don't you think you ought to get up and pray to God for a new heart?"

"Y-yess."

"Get out and pray, then!" And Punch would get out of bed with raging hate in his heart against all the world, seen and unseen. He was always tumbling into trouble. Harry had a knack of cross-examining him as to his day's doings, which seldom failed to lead him, sleepy and savage, into half a dozen contradictions—all duly reported to Aunty Rosa next morning.

"But it was n't a lie," Punch would begin, charging into a laboured explanation that landed him more hopelessly in the mire. "I said that I did n't say my prayers twice over in the day, and that was on Tuesday. Once I did, I know I did, but Harry said I did n't," and so forth, till the tension brought tears, and he was dismissed from the table in disgrace.

"You use n't to be as bad as this?" said Judy, awe-stricken at the catalogue of Black Sheep's crimes. "Why are you so bad now?"

"I don't know," Black Sheep would reply. "I 'm not, if I only was n't bothered upside down. I knew what I did, and I want to say so; but Harry always makes it out different somehow, and Aunty Rosa does n't believe a word I say. Oh, Ju! don't you say I 'm bad too."

"Aunty Rosa says you are," said Judy. "She told the Vicar so when he came yesterday."

"Why does she tell all the people outside the house about me? It is n't fair," said Black Sheep. "When I was in Bombay, and was bad—doing bad, not made-up bad like this—Mamma told Papa, and Papa told me he knew, and that was all. Outside people did n't know too—even Meeta did n't know."

"I don't remember," said Judy wistfully. "I was all little then. Mamma was just as fond of you as she was of me, was n't she?"

" 'Course she was. So was Papa. So was everybody."

"Aunty Rosa likes me more than she does you. She says that you are a Trial and a Black Sheep, and I 'm not to speak to you more than I can help."

"Always? Not outside of the times when you must n't speak to me at all?"

Judy nodded her head mournfully. Black Sheep turned away in despair, but Judy's arms were round his neck.

"Never mind, Punch," she whispered. "I will speak to you

just the same as ever and ever. You 're my own, own brother though you are—though Aunty Rosa says you 're Bad, and Harry says you 're a little coward. He says that if I pulled your hair hard, you 'd cry."

"Pull, then," said Punch.

Judy pulled gingerly.

"Pull harder—as hard as you can! There! I don't mind how much you pull it now. If you 'll speak to me same as ever I 'll let you pull it as much as you like—pull it out if you like. But I know if Harry came and stood by and made you do it I 'd cry."

So the two children sealed the compact with a kiss, and Black Sheep's heart was cheered within him, and by extreme caution and careful avoidance of Harry he acquired virtue and was allowed to read undisturbed for a week. Uncle Harry took him for walks and consoled him with rough tenderness, never calling him Black Sheep. "It 's good for you, I suppose, Punch," he used to say. "Let us sit down. I 'm getting tired." His steps led him now not to the beach, but to the Cemetery of Rocklington, amid the potato-fields. For hours the gray man would sit on a tombstone, while Black Sheep read epitaphs, and then with a sigh would stump home again.

"I shall lie there soon," said he to Black Sheep, one winter evening, when his face showed white as a worn silver coin under the lights of the chapel-lodge. "You need n't tell Aunty Rosa."

A month later, he turned sharp round, ere half a morning walk was completed, and stumped back to the house. "Put me to bed, Rosa," he muttered. "I 've walked my last. The wadding has found me out."

They put him to bed, and for a fortnight the shadow of his sickness lay upon the house, and Black Sheep went to and fro unobserved. Papa had sent him some new books, and he was told to keep quiet. He retired into his own world, and was perfectly happy. Even at night his felicity was unbroken. He could lie in bed and string himself tales of travel and adventure while Harry was downstairs.

"Uncle Harry 's going to die," said Judy, who now lived almost entirely with Aunty Rosa.

"I 'm very sorry," said Black Sheep soberly. "He told me that a long time ago."

Aunty Rosa heard the conversation. "Will nothing check your wicked tongue?" she said angrily. There were blue circles round her eyes.

Black Sheep retreated to the nursery and read "Cometh up as a Flower" with deep and uncomprehending interest. He had been forbidden to read it on account of its "sinfulness," but the bonds of the Universe were crumbling, and Aunty Rosa was in great grief.

"I 'm glad," said Black Sheep. "She 's unhappy now. It was n't a lie, though. I knew. He told me not to tell."

That night Black Sheep woke with a start. Harry was not in the room, and there was a sound of sobbing on the next floor. Then the voice of Uncle Harry, singing the song of the Battle of Navarino, cut through the darkness:

> "Our vanship was the Asia—
> The Albion and Genoa!"

"He 's getting well," thought Black Sheep, who knew the song through all its seventeen verses. But the blood froze at his little heart as he thought. The voice leapt an octave and rang shrill as a boatswain's pipe:

> "And next came on the lovely Rose,
> The Philomel, her fire-ship, closed,
> And the Little Brisk was sore exposed
> That day at Navarino."

"That day at Navarino, Uncle Harry!" shouted Black Sheep, half wild with excitement and fear of he knew not what.

A door opened and Aunty Rosa screamed up the staircase: "Hush! For God's sake hush, you little devil. Uncle Harry is dead!"

THE THIRD BAG

Journeys end in lovers' meeting,
Every wise man's son doth know.

"I wonder what will happen to me now," thought Black Sheep, when the semi-pagan rites peculiar to the burial of the Dead in middle-class houses had been accomplished, and Aunty Rosa, awful in black crape, had returned to this life. "I don't think I 've done anything bad that she knows of. I suppose I will soon. She will be very cross after Uncle Harry's dying, and Harry will be cross too. I 'll keep in the nursery."

Unfortunately for Punch's plans, it was decided that he should be sent to a day-school which Harry attended. This meant a morning walk with Harry, and perhaps an evening one; but the prospect of freedom in the interval was refreshing. "Harry 'll tell everything I do, but I won't do anything," said Black Sheep. Fortified with this virtuous resolution, he went to school only to find that Harry's version of his character had preceded him, and that life was a burden in consequence. He took stock of his associates. Some of them were unclean, some of them talked in dialect, many dropped their h's, and there were two Jews and a Negro, or someone quite as dark, in the assembly. "That 's a hubshi," said Black Sheep to himself. "Even Meeta used to laugh at a hubshi. I don't think this is a proper place." He was indignant for at least an hour, till he reflected that any expostulation on his part would be by Aunty Rosa construed into "showing off," and that Harry would tell the boys.

"How do you like school?" said Aunty Rosa at the end of the day.

"I think it is a very nice place," said Punch quietly.

"I suppose you warned the boys of Black Sheep's character?" said Aunty Rosa to Harry.

"Oh, yes!" said the censor of Black Sheep's morals. "They know all about him."

"If I was with my father," said Black Sheep, stung to the quick, "I should n't speak to those boys. He would n't let me. They live in shops. I saw them go into shops—where their fathers live and sell things."

"You 're too good for that school, are you?" said Aunty Rosa, with a bitter smile. "You ought to be grateful, Black Sheep, that those boys speak to you at all. It is n't every school that takes little liars."

Harry did not fail to make much capital out of Black Sheep's ill-considered remark; with the result that several boys, including the hubshi, demonstrated to Black Sheep the eternal equality of the human race by smacking his head, and his consolation from Aunty Rosa was that it "served him right for being vain." He learned, however, to keep his opinions to himself, and by propitiating Harry in carrying books and the like to secure a little peace. His existence was not too joyful. From nine till twelve he was at school, and from two to four, except on Saturdays. In the evenings he was sent down into the nursery to prepare his lessons for the next day, and every night came the dreaded cross-questionings at Harry's hand. Of Judy he saw but little. She was deeply religious—at six years of age Religion is easy to come by—and sorely divided between her natural love for Black Sheep and her love for Aunty Rosa, who could do no wrong.

The lean woman returned that love with interest, and Judy, when she dared, took advantage of this for the remission of Black Sheep's penalties. Failures in lessons at school were furnished at home by a week without reading other than schoolbooks, and Harry brought the news of such a failure with glee. Further, Black Sheep was then bound to repeat his lessons at bedtime to Harry, who generally succeeded in making him break down, and consoled him by gloomiest forebodings for the morrow. Harry was at once spy, practical joker, inquisitor, and Aunty Rosa's deputy executioner. He filled his many posts to admiration. From his actions, now that Uncle Harry was dead, there was no appeal. Black Sheep had not been permitted to keep any self-respect at school; at home he was of course utterly discredited, and grateful for any pity that the servant-girls—they changed frequently at Downe Lodge because they, too, were liars— might show. "You 're just fit to row in the same boat with Black Sheep," was a sentiment that each new Jane or Eliza might expect to hear, before a month was over, from Aunty Rosa's lips; and Black Sheep was used to ask new girls whether they had yet been compared to him. Harry was "Master Harry" in their mouths; Judy was officially "Miss Judy"; but Black Sheep was never anything more than Black Sheep *tout court*.

As time went on and the memory of Papa and Mamma became wholly overlaid by the unpleasant task of writing them letters under Aunty Rosa's eye, each Sunday, Black Sheep forgot what manner of life he had led in the beginning of things. Even Judy's appeals to "try and remember about Bombay" failed to quicken him.

"I can't remember," he said. "I know I used to give orders and Mamma kissed me."

"Aunty Rosa will kiss you if you are good," pleaded Judy.

"Ugh! I don't want to be kissed by Aunty Rosa. She 'd say I was doing it to get something more to eat."

The weeks lengthened into months, and the holidays came; but just before the holidays Black Sheep fell into deadly sin. Among the many boys whom Harry had incited to "punch Black Sheep's head because he dare n't hit back," was one more aggravating than the rest, who, in an unlucky moment, fell upon Black Sheep when Harry was not near. The blows stung, and Black Sheep struck back at random with all the power at his command. The boy dropped and whimpered. Black Sheep was astounded at his own act, but, feeling the unresisting body under him, shook it with both his hands in blind fury and then began to throttle his enemy; meaning honestly to slay him. There was a scuffle, and Black Sheep was torn off the body by Harry and some colleagues, and cuffed home tingling but exultant. Aunty Rosa was out; pending her arrival Harry set himself to lecture Black Sheep on the sin of murder—which he described as the offence of Cain.

"Why did n't you fight him fair? What did you hit him when he was down for, you little cur?"

Black Sheep looked up at Harry's throat and then at a knife on the dinner-table.

"I don't understand," he said wearily. "You always set him on me and told me I was a coward when I blubbed. Will you leave me alone until Aunty Rosa comes in? She 'll beat me if you tell her I ought to be beaten; so it 's all right."

"It 's all wrong," said Harry magisterially. "You nearly killed him, and I should n't wonder if he dies."

"Will he die?" said Black Sheep.

"I daresay," said Harry, "and then you 'll be hanged."

"All right," said Black Sheep, possessing himself of the table-knife. "Then I 'll kill you now. You say things and do things and—and I don't know how things happen, and you never leave me alone—and I don't care what happens!"

He ran at the boy with the knife, and Harry fled upstairs to his room, promising Black Sheep the finest thrashing in the world when Aunty Rosa returned. Black Sheep sat at the bottom of the stairs, the table-knife in his hand, and wept for that he had not killed Harry. The servant-girl came up from the kitchen, took the knife away, and consoled him. But Black Sheep was beyond consolation. He would be badly beaten by Aunty Rosa; then there would be another beating at Harry's hands; then Judy would not be allowed to speak to him; then the tale would be told at school and then——

There was no one to help and no one to care, and the best way out of the business was by death. A knife would hurt, but Aunty Rosa had told him, a year ago, that if he sucked paint he would die. He went into the nursery, unearthed the now-disused Noah's Ark, and sucked the paint off as many animals as remained. It tasted abominable, but he had licked Noah's Dove clean by the time Aunty Rosa and Judy returned. He went upstairs and greeted them with: "Please, Aunty Rosa, I believe I 've nearly killed a boy at school, and I 've tried to kill Harry, and when you 've done all about God and Hell, will you beat me and get it over?"

The tale of the assault as told by Harry could only be explained on the ground of possession by the Devil. Wherefore Black Sheep was not only most excellently beaten, once by Aunty Rosa and once, when thoroughly cowed down, by Harry, but he was further prayed for at family prayers, together with Jane, who had stolen a cold rissole from the pantry and snuffled audibly as her enormity was brought before the Throne of Grace. Black Sheep was sore and stiff, but triumphant. He would die that very night and be rid of them all. No, he would ask for no forgiveness from Harry, and at bedtime would stand no questioning at Harry's hands, even though addressed as "Young Cain."

"I 've been beaten," said he, "and I 've done other things. I don't care what I do. If you speak to me to-night, Harry, I 'll get out and try to kill you. Now you can kill me if you like."

Harry took his bed into the spare-room, and Black Sheep lay down to die.

It may be that the makers of Noah's Arks know that their animals are likely to find their way into young mouths, and paint them accordingly. Certain it is that the common, weary next morning broke through the windows and found Black Sheep quite well and a good deal ashamed of himself, but richer by the knowledge that he could, in extremity, secure himself against Harry for the future.

When he descended to breakfast on the first day of the holidays, he was greeted with the news that Harry, Aunty Rosa, and Judy were going away to Brighton, while Black Sheep was to stay in the house with the servant. His latest outbreak suited Aunty Rosa's plans admirably. It gave her good excuse for leaving the extra boy behind. Papa in Bombay, who really seemed to know a young sinner's wants to the hour, sent, that week, a package of new books. And with these, and the society of Jane on board-wages, Black Sheep was left alone for a month.

The books lasted for ten days. They were eaten too quickly, in long gulps of four-and-twenty hours at a time. Then came days of doing absolutely nothing, of dreaming dreams and marching imaginary armies up and down stairs, of counting the number of banisters, and of measuring the length and breadth of every room in handspans—fifty down the side, thirty across, and fifty back again. Jane made many friends, and, after receiving Black Sheep's assurance that he would not tell of her absences, went out daily for long hours. Black Sheep would follow the rays of the sinking sun from the kitchen to the dining-room and thence upward to his own bedroom until all was gray dark, and he ran down to the kitchen fire and read by its light. He was happy in that he was left alone and could read as much as he pleased. But, later, he grew afraid of the shadows of window-curtains and the flapping of doors and the creaking of shutters. He went out into the garden, and the rustling of the laurel-bushes frightened him.

He was glad when they all returned—Aunty Rosa, Harry, and Judy—full of news, and Judy laden with gifts. Who could help loving loyal little Judy? In return for all her merry babblement, Black Sheep confided to her that the distance from the hall-door to the top of the first landing was exactly one hundred and eighty-four handspans. He had found it out himself.

Then the old life recommenced; but with a difference, and a new sin. To his other iniquities Black Sheep had now added a phenomenal clumsiness—was as unfit to trust in action as he was in word. He himself could not account for spilling everything he touched, upsetting glasses as he put his hand out, and bumping his head against doors that were manifestly shut. There was a gray haze upon all his world, and it narrowed month by month, until at last it left Black Sheep almost alone with the flapping curtains that were so like ghosts, and the nameless terrors of broad daylight that were only coats on pegs after all.

Holidays came and holidays went, and Black Sheep was taken to see many people whose faces were all exactly alike; was beaten when occasion demanded, and tortured by Harry on all possible occasions; but defended by Judy through good and evil report, though she hereby drew upon herself the wrath of Aunty Rosa.

The weeks were interminable and Papa and Mamma were clean forgotten. Harry had left school and was a clerk in a Banking-Office. Freed from his presence, Black Sheep resolved that he should no longer be deprived of his allowance of pleasure-reading. Consequently, when he failed at school he reported that all was well, and conceived a large contempt for Aunty Rosa as he saw how easy it was to deceive her. "She says I'm a little liar when I don't tell lies, and now I do, she does n't know," thought Black Sheep. Aunty Rosa had credited him in the past with petty cunning and stratagem that had never entered into his head. By the light of the sordid knowledge that she had revealed to him he paid her back full tale. In a household where the most innocent of his motives, his natural yearning for a little affection, had been interpreted into a desire for more bread and jam or to ingratiate himself with strangers and so put Harry into the background, his work was easy. Aunty Rosa could penetrate certain kinds of hypocrisy, but not all. He set his child's wits against hers and was no more beaten. It grew monthly more and more of a trouble to read the schoolbooks, and even the pages of the open-print story-books danced and were dim. So Black Sheep brooded in the shadows that fell about him and cut him off from the world, inventing horrible punishments for "dear Harry," or plotting another line of the tangled web of deception that he wrapped round Aunty Rosa.

Then the crash came and the cobwebs were broken. It was impossible to foresee everything. Aunty Rosa made personal inquiries as to Black Sheep's progress and received information that startled her. Step by step, with a delight as keen as when she convicted an underfed housemaid of the theft of cold meats, she followed the trail of Black Sheep's delinquencies. For weeks and weeks, in order to escape banishment from the book-shelves, he had made a fool of Aunty Rosa, of Harry, of God, of all the world. Horrible, most horrible, and evidence of an utterly depraved mind.

Black Sheep counted the cost. "It will only be one big beating, and then she'll put a card with 'Liar' on my back, same as she did before. Harry will whack me and pray for me, and she will pray for me at prayers and tell me I'm a Child of the Devil and give me hymns to learn. But I've done all my reading and she never knew. She'll say she knew all along. She's an old liar, too," said he.

For three days Black Sheep was shut in his own bedroom— to prepare his heart. "That means two beatings. One at school and one here. That one will hurt most." And it fell even as he thought. He was thrashed at school before the Jews and the hubshi, for the heinous crime of bringing home false reports of progress. He was thrashed at home by Aunty Rosa on the same count, and then the placard was produced. Aunty Rosa stitched it between his shoulders and bade him go for a walk with it upon him.

"If you make me do that," said Black Sheep very quietly, "I shall burn this house down, and perhaps I'll kill you. I don't know whether I can kill you—you're so bony—but I'll try."

No punishment followed this blasphemy, though Black Sheep held himself ready to work his way to Aunty Rosa's withered throat, and grip there till he was beaten off. Perhaps Aunty Rosa was afraid, for Black Sheep, having reached the Nadir of Sin, bore himself with a new recklessness.

In the midst of all the trouble there came a visitor from over the seas to Downe Lodge, who knew Papa and Mamma, and was commissioned to see Punch and Judy. Black Sheep was sent to the drawing-room and charged into a solid tea-table laden with china.

"Gently, gently, little man," said the visitor, turning Black Sheep's face to the light slowly. "What's that big bird on the palings?"

"What bird?" asked Black Sheep.

The visitor looked deep down into Black Sheep's eyes for a half a minute, and then said suddenly: "Good God, the little chap's nearly blind."

It was a most business-like visitor. He gave orders, on his own responsibility, that Black Sheep was not to go to school or open a book until Mamma came home. "She'll be here in three weeks, as you know of course," said he, "and I'm Inverarity Sahib. I ushered you into this wicked world, young man, and a nice use you seem to have made of your time. You must do nothing whatever. Can you do that?"

"Yes," said Punch in a dazed way. He had known that Mamma was coming. There was a chance, then, of another beating. Thank Heaven, Papa wasn't coming too. Aunty Rosa had said of late that he ought to be beaten by a man.

For the next three weeks Black Sheep was strictly allowed to do nothing. He spent his time in the old nursery looking at the broken toys, for all of which account must be rendered to Mamma. Aunty Rosa hit him over the hands if even a wooden boat were broken. But that sin was of small importance compared to the other revelations, so darkly hinted at by Aunty Rosa. "When your mother comes, and hears what I have to tell her, she may appreciate you properly," she said grimly, and mounted guard over Judy lest that small maiden should attempt to comfort her brother, to the peril of her own soul.

And Mamma came—in a four-wheeler and a flutter of tender excitement. Such a Mamma! She was young, frivolously young, and beautiful, with delicately flushed cheeks, eyes that shone like stars, and a voice that needed no additional appeal of outstretched arms to draw little ones to her heart. Judy ran straight to her, but Black Sheep hesitated. Could this wonder be "showing off"? She would not put out her arms when she knew of his crimes. Meantime was it possible that by fondling she wanted to get anything out of Black Sheep? Only all his love and all his confidence; but that Black Sheep did not know. Aunty Rosa withdrew and left Mamma, kneeling between her children, half laughing, half crying, in the very hall where Punch and Judy had wept five years before.

"Well, chicks, do you remember me?"

"No," said Judy frankly, "but I said 'God bless Papa and Mamma,' ev'vy night."

"A little," said Black Sheep. "Remember I wrote to you every week, anyhow. That is n't to show off, but 'cause of what comes afterward."

"What comes after! What should come after, my darling boy?" And she drew him to her again. He came awkwardly, with many angles. "Not used to petting," said the quick Mother-soul. "The girl is."

"She 's too little to hurt anyone," thought Black Sheep, "and if I said I 'd kill her, she 'd be afraid. I wonder what Aunty Rosa will tell."

There was a constrained late dinner, at the end of which Mamma picked up Judy and put her to bed with endearments manifold. Faithless little Judy had shown her defection from Aunty Rosa already. And that lady resented it bitterly. Black Sheep rose to leave the room.

"Come and say good night," said Aunty Rosa, offering a withered cheek.

"Huh!" said Black Sheep. "I never kiss you, and I 'm not

going to show off. Tell that woman what I 've done, and see
what she says."

Black Sheep climbed into bed feeling that he had lost
Heaven after a glimpse through the gates. In half an hour
"that woman" was bending over him. Black Sheep flung up
his right arm. It was n't fair to come and hit him in the dark.
Even Aunty Rosa never tried that. But no blow followed.

"Are you showing off? I won't tell you anything more than
Aunty Rosa has, and she does n't know everything," said
Black Sheep as clearly as he could for the arms round his
neck.

"Oh, my son—my little, little son! It was my fault—my
fault, darling—and yet how could we help it? Forgive me,
Punch." The voice died out in a broken whisper, and two hot
tears fell on Black Sheep's forehead.

"Has she been making you cry, too?" he asked. "You
should see Jane cry. But you 're nice, and Jane is a Born Liar
—Aunty Rosa says so."

"Hush, Punch, hush! My boy, don't talk like that. Try to
love me a little bit—a little bit. You don't know how I want
it. Punch-baba, come back to me! I am your Mother—your
own Mother—and never mind the rest. I know—yes, I know,
dear. It does n't matter now. Punch, won't you care for me
a little?"

It is astonishing how much petting a big boy of ten can
endure when he is quite sure that there is no one to laugh at
him. Black Sheep had never been made much of before, and
here was this beautiful woman treating him—Black Sheep,
the Child of the Devil and the Inheritor of Undying Flame—
as though he were a small God.

"I care for you a great deal, Mother dear," he whispered
at last, "and I 'm glad you 've come back; but are you sure
Aunty Rosa told you everything?"

"Everything. What does it matter? But——" the voice broke with a sob that was also laughter—"Punch, my poor, dear, half-blind darling, don't you think it was a little foolish of you?"

"No. It saved a lickin'."

Mamma shuddered and slipped away in the darkness to write a long letter to Papa. Here is an extract:

". . . Judy is a dear, plump little prig who adores the woman, and wears with as much gravity as her religious opinions—only eight, Jack!—a venerable horsehair atrocity which she calls her Bustle. I have just burned it, and the child is asleep in my bed as I write. She will come to me at once. Punch I cannot quite understand. He is well nourished, but seems to have been worried into a system of small deceptions which the woman magnifies into deadly sins. Don't you recollect our own up-bringing, dear, when the Fear of the Lord was so often the beginning of falsehood? I shall win Punch to me before long. I am taking the children away into the country to get them to know me, and, on the whole, I am content, or shall be when you come home, dear boy, and then, thank God, we shall be all under one roof again at last!"

Three months later, Punch, no longer Black Sheep, has discovered that he is the veritable owner of a real, live, lovely Mamma, who is also a sister, comforter, and friend, and that he must protect her till the Father comes home. Deception does not suit the part of a protector, and, when one can do anything without question, where is the use of deception?

"Mother would be awfully cross if you walked through that ditch," says Judy, continuing a conversation.

"Mother's never angry," says Punch. "She'd just say, 'You're a little pagal'; and that's not nice, but I'll show."

Punch walks through the ditch and mires himself to the knees. "Mother, dear," he shouts, "I 'm just as dirty as I can pos-sib-ly be!"

"Then change your clothes as quickly as you pos-sib-ly can!" rings out Mother's clear voice from the house. "And don't be a little pagal!"

"There! Told you so," says Punch. "It 's all different now, and we are just as much Mother 's as if she had never gone."

Not altogether, O Punch, for when young lips have drunk deep of the bitter waters of Hate, Suspicion, and Despair, all the Love in the world will not wholly take away that knowledge; though it may turn darkened eyes for a while to the light, and teach Faith where no Faith was.

XV

A SELECTION FROM "MOWGLI'S BROTHERS"

From *The Jungle Book*

IT WAS seven o'clock of a very warm evening in the Seeonee hills when Father Wolf woke up from his day's rest, scratched himself, yawned, and spread out his paws one after the other to get rid of the sleepy feeling in the tips. Mother Wolf lay with her big gray nose dropped across her four tumbling, squealing cubs, and the moon shone into the mouth of the cave where they all lived. "Augrh!" said Father Wolf, "it is time to hunt again"; and he was going to spring downhill when a little shadow with a bushy tail crossed the threshold and whined: "Good luck go with you, O Chief of the Wolves; and good luck and strong white teeth go with the noble children, that they may never forget the hungry in this world."

It was the jackal—Tabaqui, the Dish-licker—and the wolves of India despise Tabaqui because he runs about making mischief, and telling tales, and eating rags and pieces of leather from the village rubbish-heaps. They are afraid of him too, because Tabaqui, more than any one else in the jungle, is apt to go mad, and then he forgets that he was ever afraid of any one, and runs through the forest biting everything in his way. Even the tiger hides when little Tabaqui goes mad, for madness is the most disgraceful thing that can overtake a wild creature. We call it hydrophobia, but they call it *dewanee*—the madness—and run.

"Enter, then, and look," said Father Wolf, stiffly; "but there is no food here."

"For a wolf, no," said Tabaqui; "but for so mean a person as myself a dry bone is a good feast. Who are we, the Gidurlog [the Jackal People], to pick and choose?" He scuttled to the back of the cave, where he found the bone of a buck with some meat on it, and sat cracking the end merrily.

"All thanks for this good meal," he said, licking his lips. "How beautiful are the noble children! How large are their eyes! And so young too! Indeed, indeed, I might have remembered that the children of kings are men from the beginning."

Now, Tabaqui knew as well as any one else that there is nothing so unlucky as to compliment children to their faces; and it pleased him to see Mother and Father Wolf look uncomfortable.

Tabaqui sat still, rejoicing in the mischief that he had made, and then he said spitefully:

"Shere Khan, the Big One, has shifted his hunting-grounds. He will hunt among these hills during the next moon, so he has told me."

Shere Khan was the tiger who lived near the Waingunga River, twenty miles away.

"He has no right!" Father Wolf began angrily. "By the Law of the Jungle he has no right to change his quarters without fair warning. He will frighten every head of game within ten miles; and I—I have to kill for two, these days."

"His mother did not call him Lungri [the Lame One] for nothing," said Mother Wolf, quietly. "He has been lame in one foot from his birth. That is why he has only killed cattle. Now the villagers of the Waingunga are angry with him, and he has come here to make *our* villagers angry. They will scour the jungle for him when he is far away, and we and our children must run when the grass is set alight. Indeed, we are very grateful to Shere Khan!"

"Shall I tell him of your gratitude?" said Tabaqui.

"Out!" snapped Father Wolf. "Out, and hunt with thy master. Thou hast done harm enough for one night."

"I go," said Tabaqui, quietly. "Ye can hear Shere Khan below in the thickets. I might have saved myself the message."

Father Wolf listened, and in the dark valley that ran down to a little river, he heard the dry, angry, snarly, singsong whine of a tiger who has caught nothing and does not care if all the jungle knows it.

"The fool!" said Father Wolf. "To begin a night's work with that noise! Does he think that our buck are like his fat Waingunga bullocks?"

It pleased him to see Mother and Father Wolf look uncomfortable.

"H'sh! It is neither bullock nor buck that he hunts to-night," said Mother Wolf; "it is Man." The whine had changed to a sort of humming purr that seemed to roll from every quarter of the compass. It was the noise that bewilders wood-cutters, and gipsies sleeping in the open, and makes them run sometimes into the very mouth of the tiger.

"Man!" said Father Wolf, showing all his white teeth. "Faugh! Are there not enough beetles and frogs in the tanks that he must eat Man—and on our ground too!"

The Law of the Jungle, which never orders anything without a reason, forbids every beast to eat Man except when he is killing to show his children how to kill, and then he must hunt outside the hunting-grounds of his pack or tribe. The real reason for this is that man-killing means, sooner or later, the arrival of white men on elephants, with guns, and hundreds of brown men with gongs and rockets and torches. Then everybody in the jungle suffers. The reason the beasts give among themselves is that Man is the weakest and most defenseless of all living things, and it is unsportsmanlike to touch him. They say too—and it is true—that man-eaters become mangy, and lose their teeth.

The purr grew louder, and ended in the full-throated "Aaarh!" of the tiger's charge.

Then there was a howl—an untigerish howl—from Shere Khan. "He has missed," said Mother Wolf. "What is it?"

Father Wolf ran out a few paces and heard Shere Khan muttering and mumbling savagely, as he tumbled about in the scrub.

"The fool has had no more sense than to jump at a wood-cutter's camp-fire, so he has burned his feet," said Father Wolf, with a grunt. "Tabaqui is with him."

"Something is coming uphill," said Mother Wolf, twitching one ear. "Get ready."

The bushes rustled a little in the thicket, and Father Wolf dropped with his haunches under him, ready for his leap. Then, if you had been watching, you would have seen the most wonderful thing in the world—the wolf checked in mid-spring. He made his bound before he saw what it was he was jumping at, and then he tried to stop himself. The result was that he shot up straight into the air for four or five feet, landing almost where he left ground.

"Man!" he snapped. "A man's cub. Look!"

Directly in front of him, holding on by a low branch, stood a naked brown baby who could just walk, as soft and as dimpled a little thing as ever came to a wolf's cave at night. He looked up into Father Wolf's face and laughed.

"Is that a man's cub?" said Mother Wolf. "I have never seen one. Bring it here."

A wolf accustomed to moving his own cubs can, if necessary, mouth an egg without breaking it, and though Father Wolf's jaws closed right on the child's back not a tooth even scratched the skin, as he laid it down among the cubs.

"How little! How naked, and—how bold!" said Mother Wolf, softly. The baby was pushing his way between the cubs to get close to the warm hide. "Ahai! He is taking his meal with the others. And so this is a man's cub. Now was there ever a wolf that could boast of a man's cub among her children?"

"I have heard now and again of such a thing, but never in our pack or in my time," said Father Wolf. "He is altogether without hair, and I could kill him with a touch of my foot. But see, he looks up and is not afraid."

The moonlight was blocked out of the mouth of the cave, for Shere Khan's great square head and shoulders were thrust into the entrance, Tabaqui, behind him, was squeaking: "My Lord, my Lord, it went in here!"

"Shere Khan does us great honour," said Father Wolf, but his eyes were very angry. "What does Shere Khan need?"

"My quarry. A man's cub went this way," said Shere Khan. "Its parents have run off. Give it to me."

Shere Khan had jumped at a wood-cutter's camp-fire, as Father Wolf had said, and was furious from the pain of his burned feet. But Father Wolf knew that the mouth of the cave was too narrow for a tiger to come in by. Even where he was, Shere Khan's shoulders and fore paws were cramped for want of room, as a man's would be if he tried to fight in a barrel.

"The Wolves are a free people," said Father Wolf. "They take orders from the Head of the Pack, and not from any striped cattle-killer. The man's cub is ours—to kill if we choose."

"Ye choose and ye do not choose! What talk is this of choosing? By the Bull that I killed, am I to stand nosing into your dog's den for my fair dues? It is I, Shere Khan, who speak!"

The tiger's roar filled the cave with thunder. Mother Wolf shook herself clear of the cubs and sprang forward, her eyes, like two green moons in the darkness, facing the blazing eyes of Shere Khan.

"And it is I, Raksha [the Demon], who answer. The man's cub is mine, Lungri—mine to me! He shall not be killed. He shall live to run with the Pack and to hunt with the Pack; and in the end, look you, hunter of little naked cubs—frog-eater—fish-killer, shall hunt *thee!* Now get hence, or by the

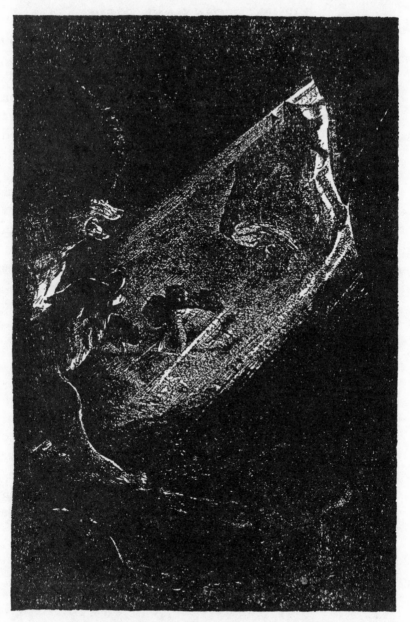

"A man's cub went this way," said Shere Khan.

Sambhur that I killed (I eat no starved cattle), back thou goest to thy mother, burned beast of the jungle, lamer than ever thou camest into the world! Go!"

Father Wolf looked on amazed. He had almost forgotten the days when he won Mother Wolf in fair fight from five other wolves, when she ran in the Pack and was not called the Demon for compliment's sake. Shere Khan might have faced Father Wolf, but he could not stand up against Mother Wolf, for he knew that where he was she had all the advantage of the ground, and would fight to the death. So he backed out of the cave-mouth growling, and when he was clear he shouted:

"Each dog barks in his own yard! We will see what the Pack will say to this fostering of man-cubs. The cub is mine, and to my teeth he will come in the end, O bush-tailed thieves!"

Mother Wolf threw herself down panting among the cubs, and Father Wolf said to her gravely:

"Shere Khan speaks this much truth. The cub must be shown to the Pack. Wilt thou still keep him, Mother?"

"Keep him!" she gasped. "He came naked, by night, alone and very hungry; yet he was not afraid! Look, he has pushed one of my babes to one side already. And that lame butcher would have killed him, and would have run off to the Waingunga while the villagers here hunted through all our lairs in revenge! Keep him? Assuredly I will keep him. Lie still, little frog. O thou Mowgli,—for Mowgli, the Frog, I will call thee, —the time will come when thou wilt hunt Shere Khan as he has hunted thee!"

"But what will our Pack say?" said Father Wolf.

The Law of the Jungle lays down very clearly that any wolf may, when he marries, withdraw from the Pack he belongs to; but as soon as his cubs are old enough to stand on their feet he must bring them to the Pack Council, which is generally held once a month at full moon, in order that the other wolves may identify them. After that inspection the cubs are free to run where they please, and until they have killed their first buck no excuse is accepted if a grown wolf of the Pack kills one of them. The punishment is death where the murderer can be found; and if you think for a minute you will see that this must be so.

Father Wolf waited till his cubs could run a little, and then on the night of the Pack Meeting took them and Mowgli and Mother Wolf to the Council Rock—a hilltop covered with stones and boulders where a hundred wolves could hide. Akela, the great gray Lone Wolf, who led all the Pack by strength and cunning, lay out at full length on his rock, and below him sat forty or more wolves of every size and colour, from badger-coloured veterans who could handle a buck alone, to young black three-year-olds who thought they could. The Lone Wolf had led them for a year now. He had fallen twice into a wolf-trap in his youth, and once he had been beaten and left for dead; so he knew the manners and customs of men.

There was very little talking at the Rock. The cubs tumbled over one another in the center of the circle where their mothers and fathers sat, and now and again a senior wolf would go quietly up to a cub, look at him carefully, and return to his place on noiseless feet. Sometimes a mother would push her cub far out into the moonlight, to be sure that he had not been overlooked. Akela from his rock would cry: "Ye know the Law—ye know the Law! Look well, O Wolves!" And the anxious mothers would take up the call: "Look—look well, O Wolves!"

At last—and Mother Wolf's neck-bristles lifted as the time came—Father Wolf pushed "Mowgli, the Frog," as they called him, into the center, where he sat laughing and playing with some pebbles that glistened in the moonlight.

Akela never raised his head from his paws, but went on with the monotonous cry, "Look well!" A muffled roar came up from behind the rocks—the voice of Shere Khan crying, "The cub is mine; give him to me. What have the Free People to do with a man's cub?"

Akela never even twitched his ears. All he said was, "Look well, O Wolves! What have the Free People to do with the orders of any save the Free People? Look well!"

There was a chorus of deep growls, and a young wolf in his fourth year flung back Shere Khan's question to Akela: "What have the Free People to do with a man's cub?"

Now the Law of the Jungle lays down that if there is any dispute as to the right of a cub to be accepted by the Pack, he must be spoken for by at least two members of the Pack who are not his father and mother.

"Who speaks for this cub?" said Akela. "Among the Free People, who speaks?" There was no answer, and Mother Wolf got ready for what she knew would be her last fight, if things came to fighting.

Then the only other creature who is allowed at the Pack Council—Baloo, the sleepy brown bear who teaches the wolf cubs the Law of the Jungle, old Baloo—who can come and go where he pleases because he eats only nuts and roots and honey—rose up on his hind quarters and grunted.

"The man's cub—the man's cub?" he said. "*I* speak for the man's cub. There is no harm in a man's cub. I have no gift of words, but I speak the truth. Let him run with the Pack, and be entered with the others. I myself will teach him."

"We need yet another," said Akela. "Baloo has spoken, and he is our teacher for the young cubs. Who speaks besides Baloo?"

A black shadow dropped down into the circle. It was Bagheera, the Black Panther, inky black all over, but with the panther markings showing up in certain lights like the pattern of watered silk. Everybody knew Bagheera, and nobody cared to cross his path; for he was as cunning as Tabaqui, as bold as the wild buffalo, and as reckless as the wounded elephant. But he had a voice as soft as wild honey dripping from a tree, and a skin softer than down.

"O Akela, and ye, the Free People," he purred, "I have no right in your assembly; but the Law of the Jungle says that if there is a doubt which is not a killing matter in regard to a new cub, the life of that cub may be bought at a price. And the Law does not say who may or may not pay that price. Am I right?"

"Good! good!" said the young wolves, who are always hungry. "Listen to Bagheera. The cub can be bought for a price. It is the Law."

"Knowing that I have no right to speak here, I ask your leave."

"Speak then," cried twenty voices.

"To kill a naked cub is shame. Besides, he may make better sport for you when he is grown. Baloo has spoken in his behalf. Now to Baloo's word I will add one bull, and a fat one, newly killed, not half a mile from here, if ye will accept the man's cub according to the Law. Is it difficult?"

There was a clamour of scores of voices, saying:

"What matter? He will die in the winter rains. He will scorch in the sun. What harm can a naked frog do us? Let him run with the Pack. Where is the bull, Bagheera? Let him be accepted." And then came Akela's deep bay, crying: "Look well—look well, O Wolves!"

Mowgli was still playing with the pebbles, and he did not notice when the wolves came and looked at him one by one. At last they all went down the hill for the dead bull, and only Akela, Bagheera, Baloo, and Mowgli's own wolves were left. Shere Khan roared still in the night, for he was very angry that Mowgli had not been handed over to him.

"Ay, roar well," said Bagheera, under his whiskers; "for the time comes when this naked thing will make thee roar to another tune, or I know nothing of Man."

"It was well done," said Akela. "Men and their cubs are very wise. He may be a help in time."

"Truly, a help in time of need; for none can hope to lead the Pack forever," said Bagheera.

Akela said nothing. He was thinking of the time that comes to every leader of every pack when his strength goes from him and he gets feebler and feebler, till at last he is killed by the wolves and a new leader comes up—to be killed in his turn.

"Take him away," he said to Father Wolf, "and train him as befits one of the Free People."

And that is how Mowgli was entered into the Seeonee wolf-pack for the price of a bull and on Baloo's good word.

Now you must be content to skip ten or eleven whole years, and only guess at all the wonderful life that Mowgli led among the wolves, because if it were written out it would fill ever so many books. He grew up with the cubs, though they of course were grown wolves almost before he was a child, and Father Wolf taught him his business, and the meaning of things in the jungle, till every rustle in the grass, every breath of the warm night air, every note of the owls above his head, every scratch of a bat's claws as it roosted for a while in a tree, and every splash of every little fish jumping in a pool, meant just as much to him as the work of his office means to a business man. When he was not learning he sat out in the sun and slept, and ate, and went to sleep again; when he felt dirty or hot he swam in the forest pools; and when he wanted honey (Baloo told him that honey and nuts were just as pleasant to eat as raw meat) he climbed up for it, and that Bagheera showed him how to do.

Bagheera would lie out on a branch and call, "Come along, Little Brother," and at first Mowgli would cling like the sloth, but afterward he would fling himself through the branches almost as boldly as the gray ape. He took his place at the Council Rock, too, when the Pack met, and there he discovered that if he stared hard at any wolf, the wolf would be forced to drop his eyes, and so he used to stare for fun.

At other times he would pick the long thorns out of the pads of his friends, for wolves suffer terribly from thorns and burrs in their coats. He would go down the hillside into the cultivated lands by night, and look very curiously at the villagers in their huts, but he had a mistrust of men because Bagheera showed him a square box with a drop-gate so cunningly hidden in the jungle that he nearly walked into it, and told him it was a trap.

He loved better than anything else to go with Bagheera into the dark, warm heart of the forest, to sleep all through the drowsy day, and at night see how Bagheera did his killing. Bagheera killed right and left as he felt hungry, and so did Mowgli—with one exception. As soon as he was old enough to understand things, Bagheera told him that he must never touch cattle because he had been bought into the Pack at the price of a bull's life. "All the jungle is thine," said Bagheera, "and thou canst kill everything that thou art strong enough to kill; but for the sake of the bull that bought thee thou must never kill or eat any cattle young or old. That is the Law of the Jungle." Mowgli obeyed faithfully.

And he grew and grew strong as a boy must grow who does not know that he is learning any lessons, and who has nothing in the world to think of except things to eat.

XVI

MOWGLI AMONG THE MONKEYS

From *The Jungle Book*

WHEN THE BEAR IS A TEACHER

LISTEN, man-cub," said the bear, and his voice rumbled like thunder on a hot night. "I have taught thee all the Law of the Jungle for all the Peoples of the Jungle, except the Monkey Folk who live in the trees. They have no law. They are outcastes. They have no speech of their own, but use the stolen words which they overhear when they listen and peep and wait up above in the branches. Their way is not our way. They are without leaders. They have no remembrance. They boast and chatter and pretend that they are a great people about to do great affairs in the jungle, but the falling of a nut turns their minds to laughter, and all is forgotten. We of the jungle have no dealings with them. We do not drink where the monkeys drink; we do not go where the monkeys go; we do not hunt where they hunt; we do not die where they die. Hast thou ever heard me speak of the Bandar-log till to-day?"

"No," said Mowgli in a whisper, for the forest was very still now that Baloo had finished.

"The Jungle People put them out of their mouths and out of their minds. They are very many, evil, dirty, shameless, and they desire, if they have any fixed desire, to be noticed by the Jungle People. But we do *not* notice them even when they throw nuts and filth on our heads."

He had hardly spoken when a shower of nuts and twigs spattered down through the branches; and they could hear coughings and howlings and angry jumpings high up in the air among the thin branches.

"The Monkey People are forbidden," said Baloo, "forbidden to the Jungle People. Remember."

"Forbidden," said Bagheera; "but I still think Baloo should have warned thee against them."

"I—I? How was I to guess he would play with such dirt. The Monkey People! Faugh!"

A fresh shower came down on their heads, and the two trotted away, taking Mowgli with them. What Baloo had said about the monkeys was perfectly true. They belonged to the tree-tops, and as beasts very seldom look up, there was no occasion for the monkeys and the Jungle People to cross one another's path. But whenever they found a sick wolf, or a wounded tiger or bear, the monkeys would torment him, and would throw sticks and nuts at any beast for fun and in the

The strongest monkeys swung off with him through the tree-tops.

hope of being noticed. Then they would howl and shriek senseless songs, and invite the Jungle People to climb up their trees and fight them, or would start furious battles over nothing among themselves, and leave the dead monkeys where the Jungle People could see them.

They were always just going to have a leader and laws and customs of their own, but they never did, because their memories would not hold over from day to day, and so they settled things by making up a saying: "What the Bandar-log think now the Jungle will think later"; and that comforted them a great deal. None of the beasts could reach them, but on the other hand none of the beasts would notice them, and that was why they were so pleased when Mowgli came to play with them, and when they heard how angry Baloo was.

They never meant to do any more—the Bandar-log never mean anything at all—but one of them invented what seemed to him a brilliant idea, and he told all the others that Mowgli would be a useful person to keep in the tribe, because he could weave sticks together for protection from the wind; so, if they caught him, they could make him teach them. Of course Mowgli, as a wood-cutter's child, inherited all sorts of instincts, and used to make little play-huts of fallen branches without thinking how he came to do it. The Monkey People, watching in the trees, considered these huts most wonderful. This time, they said, they were really going to have a leader and become the wisest people in the jungle—so wise that every one else would notice and envy them. Therefore they followed Baloo and Bagheera and Mowgli through the jungle very quietly till it was time for the midday nap, and Mowgli, who was very much ashamed of himself, slept between the panther and the bear, resolving to have no more to do with the Monkey People.

The next thing he remembered was feeling hands on his

legs and arms—hard, strong little hands—and then a swash of branches in his face; and then he was staring down through the swaying boughs as Baloo woke the jungle with his deep cries and Bagheera bounded up the trunk with every tooth bared. The Bandar-log howled with triumph, and scuffled away to the upper branches where Bagheera dared not follow, shouting: "He has noticed us! Bagheera has noticed us! All the Jungle People admire us for our skill and our cunning!" Then they began their flight; and the flight of the Monkey People through tree-land is one of the things nobody can describe. They have their regular roads and cross-roads, uphills and downhills, all laid out from fifty to seventy or a hundred feet above ground, and by these they can travel even at night if necessary.

Two of the strongest monkeys caught Mowgli under the arms and swung off with him through the tree-tops, twenty feet at a bound. Had they been alone they could have gone twice as fast, but the boy's weight held them back. Sick and giddy as Mowgli was he could not help enjoying the wild rush, though the glimpses of earth far down below frightened him, and the terrible check and jerk at the end of the swing over nothing but empty air brought his heart between his teeth.

His escort would rush him up a tree till he felt the weak topmost branches crackle and bend under them, and, then, with a cough and a whoop, would fling themselves into the air outward and downward, and bring up hanging by their hands or their feet to the lower limbs of the next tree. Sometimes he could see for miles and miles over the still green jungle, as a man on the top of a mast can see for miles across the sea, and then the branches and leaves would lash him across the face, and he and his two guards would be almost down to earth again.

So bounding and crashing and whooping and yelling, the whole tribe of Bandar-log swept along the tree-roads with Mowgli their prisoner.

For a time he was afraid of being dropped; then he grew angry, but he knew better than to struggle; and then he began to think. The first thing was to send back word to Baloo and Bagheera, for, at the pace the monkeys were going, he knew his friends would be left far behind. It was useless to look down, for he could see only the top sides of the branches, so he stared upward, and saw, far away in the blue, Rann, the Kite, balancing and wheeling as he kept watch over the jungle waiting for things to die. Rann noticed that the monkeys were carrying something, and dropped a few hundred yards to find out whether their load was good to eat. He whistled with surprise when he saw Mowgli being dragged up to a tree-top, and heard him give the Kite call for "We be of one blood, thou and I." The waves of the branches closed over the boy, but Rann balanced away to the next tree in time to see the little brown face come up again. "Mark my trail!" Mowgli shouted. "Tell Baloo of the Seeonee Pack, and Bagheera of the Council Rock."

"In whose name, Brother?" Rann had never seen Mowgli before, though of course he had heard of him.

"Mowgli, the Frog. Man-cub they call me! Mark my tra—il!"

The last words were shrieked as he was being swung through the air, but Rann nodded, and rose up till he looked no bigger than a speck of dust, and there he hung, watching with his telescope eyes the swaying of the tree-tops as Mowgli's escort whirled along.

"They never go far," he said, with a chuckle. "They never do what they set out to do. Always pecking at new things are the Bandar-log. This time, if I have any eyesight, they have

Baloo clasped his paws over his ears and rolled to and fro, moaning.

pecked down trouble for themselves, for Baloo is no fledgling, and Bagheera can, as I know, kill more than goats."

Then he rocked on his wings, his feet gathered up under him, and waited.

Meanwhile, Baloo and Bagheera were furious with rage and grief. Bagheera climbed as he had never climbed before, but the branches broke beneath his weight, and he slipped down, his claws full of bark.

"Why didst thou not warn the man-cub!" he roared to poor Baloo, who had set off at a clumsy trot in the hope of overtaking the monkeys.

"What was the use of half slaying him with blows if thou didst not warn him?"

"Haste! O haste! We—we may catch them yet!" Baloo panted.

"At that speed! It would not tire a wounded cow. Teacher of the Law, cub-beater—a mile of that rolling to and fro would burst thee open. Sit still and think! Make a plan. This is no time for chasing. They may drop him if we follow too close."

"*Arrula! Whoo!* They may have dropped him already, being tired of carrying him. Who can trust the Bandar-log? Put dead bats on my head! Give me black bones to eat! Roll me into the hives of the wild bees that I may be stung to death, and bury me with the hyena; for I am the most miserable of bears! *Arulala! Wahooa!* O Mowgli, Mowgli! Why did I not warn thee against the Monkey Folk instead of breaking thy head? Now perhaps I may have knocked the day's lesson out of his mind, and he will be alone in the jungle without the Master Words!"

Baloo clasped his paws over his ears and rolled to and fro, moaning.

"At least he gave me all the Words correctly a little time

ago," said Bagheera impatiently. "Baloo, thou hast neither memory nor respect. What would the jungle think if I, the Black Panther, curled myself up like Ikki, the Porcupine, and howled?"

"What do I care what the jungle thinks? He may be dead by now."

"Unless and until they drop him from the branches in sport, or kill him out of idleness, I have no fear for the man-cub. He is wise and well-taught, and, above all, he has the eyes that make the Jungle People afraid. But (and it is a great evil) he is in the power of the Bandar-log, and they, because they live in trees, have no fear of any of our people." Bagheera licked his one forepaw thoughtfully.

"Fool that I am! Oh fat, brown, root-digging fool that I am!" said Baloo, uncoiling himself with a jerk. "It is true what Hathi, the Wild Elephant, says: *'To each his own fear';* and they, the Bandar-log, fear Kaa, the Rock Snake. He can climb as well as they can. He steals the young monkeys in the night. The mere whisper of his name makes their wicked tails cold. Let us go to Kaa."

XVII

THE SONG THAT TOOMAI'S MOTHER
SANG TO THE BABY

From *The Jungle Book*

S HIV, who poured the harvest and made the winds to blow,
  Sitting at the doorways of a day of long ago,
Gave to each his portion, food and toil and fate,
From the King upon the *guddee* to the Beggar at the gate.
  All things made he—Shiva the Preserver.
  Mahadeo! Mahadeo! he made all—
  Thorn for the camel, fodder for the kine,
  And mother's heart for sleepy head, O little son of mine!

Wheat he gave to rich folk, millet to the poor,
Broken scraps for holy men that beg from door to door;
Cattle to the tiger, carrion to the kite,
And rags and bones to wicked wolves without the wall at
    night.
Naught he found too lofty, none he saw too low—
Parbati beside him watched them come and go;
Thought to cheat her husband, turning Shiv to jest—
Stole the little grasshopper and hid it in her breast.

So she tricked him, Shiva the Preserver.
Mahadeo! Mahadeo! turn and see.
Tall are the camels, heavy are the kine,
But this was least of little things, O little son of mine!

When the dole was ended, laughingly she said,
"Master, of a million mouths is not one unfed?"
Laughing, Shiv made answer, "All have had their part,
Even he, the little one, hidden 'neath thy heart."
From her breast she plucked it, Parbati the thief,
Saw the Least of Little Things gnawed a new-grown leaf!
Saw and feared and wondered, making prayer to Shiv,
Who hath surely given meat to all that live.
   All things made he—Shiva the Preserver.
   Mahadeo! Mahadeo! he made all—
   Thorn for the camel, fodder for the kine,
   And mother's heart for sleepy head, O little son of mine!

*"Let the tiger turn tail—in the name of the Empress,
the Overland Mail!"*

XVIII

THE OVERLAND MAIL

From *Departmental Ditties and Ballads and Barrack-Room Ballads*

IN THE name of the Empress of India, make way,
  Oh, Lords of the Jungle, wherever you roam!
The woods are astir at the close of the day—
  We exiles are waiting for letters from Home.
Let the robber retreat—let the tiger turn tail—
In the name of the Empress, the Overland Mail!

With a jingle of bells as the dusk gathers in,
  He turns to the foot-path that heads uphill—

The bag 's on his back and a cloth round his chin,
  And, tucked in his waist-belt, the Post-Office bill—
"Dispatched on this date, as received by the rail,
Per runner, two bags of the Overland Mail."

Is the torrent in spate? He must ford it or swim.
  Has the rain wrecked the road? He must climb by the cliff.
Does the tempest cry "Halt"? What are tempests to him?
  The Service admits not a "but" or an "if."
While the breath 's in his mouth, he must bear without fail,
In the name of the Empress, the Overland Mail.

From aloe to rose-oak, from rose-oak to fir.
  From level to upland, from upland to crest,
From rice-field to rock-ridge, from rock-ridge to spur,
  Fly the soft sandaled feet, strains the brawny brown chest.

"What are tempests to him?"

From rail to ravine—to the peak from the vale—
Up, up through the night goes the Overland Mail.

There 's a speck on the hill-side, a dot on the road—
    A jingle of bells on the foot-path below—
There 's a scuffle above in the monkey's abode—
    The world is awake, and the clouds are aglow.
For the great Sun himself must attend to the hail—
"In the name of the Empress, the Overland Mail."

The farmers caught our fathers and set them to work.

XIX

THE LEGEND OF EVIL

From *Departmental Ditties and Ballads and Barrack-Room Ballads*

THIS is the sorrowful story
    Told when the twilight fails
And the monkeys walk together
    Holding each other's tails.

"Our fathers lived in the forest,
    Foolish people were they,
They went down to the cornland
    To teach the farmers to play.

"Our fathers frisked in the millet,
    Our fathers skipped in the wheat,
Our fathers hung from the branches,
    Our fathers danced in the street.

"Then came the terrible farmers,
    Nothing of play they knew,
Only . . . they caught our fathers
    And set them to labour too!

"Set them to work in the cornland
    With ploughs and sickles and flails,
Put them in mud-walled prisons
    And—cut off their beautiful tails.

"Now, we can watch our fathers,
    Sullen and bowed and old,
Stooping over the millet,
    Sharing the silly mould.

"Driving a foolish furrow,
    Mending a muddy yoke,
Sleeping in mud-walled prisons,
    Steeping their food in smoke.

"The monkeys walk together holding each other's tails."

"We may not speak to our fathers,
  For if the farmers knew
They would come up to the forest
  And set us to labour too!"

This is the horrible story
  Told as the twilight fails
And the monkeys walk together
  Holding each other's tails.

XX

THE BALLAD OF THE "CLAMPHERDOWN"

From *Departmental Ditties and Ballads and Barrack-Room Ballads*

1892

IT WAS our war-ship *Clampherdown*
  Would sweep the Channel clean,
Wherefore she kept her hatches close
When the merry Channel chops arose,
  To save the bleached Marine.

She had one bow-gun of a hundred ton,
  And a great stern-gun beside;
They dipped their noses deep in the sea,
They racked their stays and stanchions free
  In the wash of the wind-whipped tide.

It was our war-ship *Clampherdown*
  Fell in with a cruiser light
That carried the dainty Hotchkiss gun
And a pair of heels wherewith to run
  From the grip of a close-fought fight.

She opened fire at seven miles—
    As ye shoot at a bobbing cork—
And once she fired and twice she fired,
Till the bow-gun drooped like a lily tired
    That lolls upon the stalk.

"Captain, the bow-gun melts apace.
    The deck-beams break below,
'T were well to rest for an hour or twain,
And botch the shattered plates again."
    And he answered, "Make it so."

She opened fire within the mile—
    As you shoot at the flying duck—
And the great stern-gun shot fair and true,
With the heave of the ship, to the stainless blue,
    And the great stern-turret stuck.

"Captain, the turret fills with steam,
    The feed-pipes burst below—
You can hear the hiss of the helpless ram,
You can hear the twisted runners jam."
    And he answered, "Turn and go!"

It was our war-ship *Clampherdown*,
    And grimly did she roll;
Swung round to take the cruiser's fire
As the White Whale faces the Thresher's ire
    When they war by the frozen Pole.

"Captain, the shells are falling fast,
    And faster still fall we;

And it is not meet for English stock
To bide in the heart of an eight-day clock
   The death they cannot see."

"Lie down, lie down, my bold A.B.,
   We drift upon her beam;
We dare not ram, for she can run:
And dare ye fire another gun,
   And die in the peeling steam?"

It was our war-ship *Clampherdown*
   That carried an armour belt;
But fifty feet at stern and bow
Lay bare as the paunch of the purser's sow
   To the hail of the Nordenfeldt.

"Captain, they lack us through and through;
   The chilled steel bolts are swift!
We have emptied the bunkers in open sea,
Their shrapnel bursts where our coal should be.
   And he answered, "Let her drift."

It was our war-ship *Clampherdown,*
   Swung round upon the tide,
Her two dumb guns glared south and north,
And the blood and the bubbling steam ran forth,
   And she ground the cruiser's side.

"Captain," they cry, "the fight is done,
   They bid you send your sword."
And he answered, "Grapple her stern and bow.
They have asked for the steel. They shall have it now;
   Out cutlasses and board!"

It was our war-ship *Clampherdown,*
  Spewed up four hundred men;
And the scalded stokers yelped delight,
As they rolled in the waist and heard the fight,
  Stamp o'er their steel-walled pen.

They cleared the cruiser end to end
  From conning-tower to hold.
They fought as they fought in Nelson's fleet;
They were stripped to the waist, they were bare to the feet,
  As it was in the days of old.

It was the sinking *Clampherdown*
  Heaved up her battered side—
And carried a million pounds in steel,
To the cod and the corpse-fed conger-eel,
  And the scour of the Channel tide.

It was the crew of the *Clampherdown*
  Stood out to sweep the sea,
On a cruiser won from an ancient foe,
As it was in the days of long ago,
  And as it still shall be!

XXI

THE DOVE OF DACCA

From *Departmental Ditties and Ballads and Barrack-Room Ballads*

THE freed dove flew to the Rajah's tower—
    Fled from the slaughter of Moslem kings—
And the thorns have covered the city of Gaur.
    Dove—dove—oh, homing dove!
Little white traitor, with woe on thy wings!

The Rajah of Dacca rode under the wall;
    He set in his bosom a dove of flight—
"If she return, be sure that I fall."
    Dove—dove—oh, homing dove!
Pressed to his heart in the thick of the fight.

"Fire the palace, the fort, and the keep—
    Leave to the foeman no spoil at all.
In the flame of the palace lie down and sleep
    If the dove, if the dove—if the homing dove
Come and alone to the palace wall."

The Kings of the North they were scattered abroad—
    The Rajah of Dacca he slew them all.
Hot from slaughter he stooped at the ford,
    And the dove—the dove—oh, the homing dove!
She thought of her cote on the palace wall.

She opened her wings and she flew away—
    Fluttered away beyond recall;
She came to the palace at break of day.
    Dove—dove—oh, homing dove!
Flying so fast for a kingdom's fall.

The Queens of Dacca they slept in flame—
    Slept in the flame of the palace old—
To save their honour from Moslem shame.
    And the dove—the dove—oh, the homing dove!
She cooed to her young where the smoke-cloud rolled.

The Rajah of Dacca rode far and fleet,
    Followed as fast as a horse could fly,
He came and the palace was black at his feet;
    And the dove—the dove—the homing dove,
Circled alone in the stainless sky.

So the dove flew to the Rajah's tower—
    Fled from the slaughter of Moslem kings;
So the thorns covered the city of Gaur,
    And Dacca was lost for a white dove's wings.
Dove—dove—oh, homing dove,
    Dacca is lost from the roll of the kings!

XXII

THE SMOKE UPON YOUR ALTAR DIES

From *Departmental Ditties and Ballads and Barrack-Room Ballads*

(To whom it may concern.)

THE smoke upon your Altar dies,
    The flowers decay,
The Goddess of your sacrifice
    Has flown away.
What profit, then, to sing or slay
    The sacrifice from day to day?

"We know the Shrine is void," they said,
    "The Goddess flown—
Yet wreaths are on the Altar laid—
    The Altar-Stone
Is black with fumes of sacrifice,
    Albeit She has fled our eyes.

"For it may be, if still we sing
    And tend the Shrine,
Some Deity on wandering wing
    May there incline;
And, finding all in order meet,
    Stay while we worship at Her feet."

XXIII

FUZZY-WUZZY

From *Departmental Ditties and Ballads and Barrack-Room Ballads*

WE'VE fought with many men acrost the seas,
  An' some of 'em was brave an' some was not:
The Paythan an' the Zulu an' Burmese;
 But the Fuzzy was the finest o' the lot.
We never got a ha'porth's change of 'im:
 'E squatted in the scrub an' 'ocked our 'orses,
'E cut our sentries up at Sua*kim,*
 An' 'e played the cat an' banjo with our forces.

> So 'ere 's *to* you, Fuzzy-Wuzzy, at your 'ome in the
> Sowdan;
> You 're a poor benighted 'eathen, but a first-class
> fightin' man;
> We gives you your certifikit, an' if you want it signed,
> We 'll come an' 'ave a romp with you whenever you 're
> inclined.

We took our chanst among the Khyber hills,
 The Boers knocked us silly at a mile,
The Burman guv us Irriwaddy chills,
 An' a Zulu *impi* dished us up in style;

173

But all we ever got from such as they
    Was pop to what the Fuzzy made us swaller;
We 'eld our bloomin' own, the papers say,
    But man for man the Fuzzy knocked us 'oller.

      Then 'ere 's *to* you, Fuzzy-Wuzzy, an' the missis an'
          the kid,
      Our orders was to break you, an' of course we went an'
          did.
      We sloshed you with Martinis, an' it was n't 'ardly fair;
      But for all the odds agin you, Fuzzy Wuz, you bruk the
          square.

'E 'as n't got no papers of 'is own,
    'E 'as n't got no medals nor rewards,
So we must certify the skill 'e 's shown
    In usin' of 'is long two-'anded swords;
When 'e 's 'oppin' in an' out among the bush
    With 'is coffin-headed shield an' shovel-spear,
A 'appy day with Fuzzy on the rush
    Will last a 'ealthy Tommy for a year.

      So 'ere 's *to* you, Fuzzy-Wuzzy, an' your friends which
          is no more,
      If we 'ad n't lost some messmates we would 'elp you to
          deplore;
      But give an' take 's the gospel, an' we 'll call the bargain
          fair,
      For if you 'ave lost more than us, you crumpled up the
          square!

'E rushes at the smoke, when we let drive,
    An', before we know, 'e 's 'ackin' at our 'ead;

'E 's all 'ot sand an' ginger when alive,
  An' 'e 's generally shammin' when 'e 's dead.
'E 's a daisy, 'e 's a duck, 'e 's a lamb!
  'E 's a Injun-rubber idiot on the spree,
'E 's the on'y thing that does n't care a clam
  For the Regiment o' British Infantree.

> So 'ere 's *to* you, Fuzzy-Wuzzy, at your 'ome in the
>   Sowdan;
> You 're a pore benighted 'eathen but a first-class
>   fightin' man;
> An' 'ere 's *to* you, Fuzzy-Wuzzy, with your 'ayrick 'ead
>   of 'air—
> You big black boundin' beggar—for you bruk a British
>   square.

XXIV

THE ENGLISH FLAG

From *Departmental Ditties and Ballads and Barrack-Room Ballads*

WINDS of the World, give answer? They are whimpering
to and fro—
And what should they know of England who only England
know?—
The poor little street-bred people that vapour and fume and
brag,
They are lifting their heads in the stillness to yelp at the
English Flag!

Must we borrow a clout from the Boer—to plaster anew
with dirt?
An Irish liar's bandage, or an English coward's shirt?
We may not speak of England; her Flag's to sell or share.
What is the Flag of England? Winds of the World, declare!

The North Wind blew:—"From Bergen my steel-shod van-
guards go;
I chase your lazy whalers home from the Disko floe;
By the great North Lights above me I work the will of God,
That the liner splits on the ice-field or the Dogger fills with
cod.

"I barred my gates with iron, I shuttered my doors with
    flame,
Because to force my ramparts your nutshell navies came;
I took the sun from their presence, I cut them down with
    my blast,
And they died, but the Flag of England blew free ere the
    spirit passed.

"The lean white bear hath seen it in the long, long Arctic
    night,
The musk-ox knows the standard that flouts the Northern
    Light:
What is the Flag of England? Ye have but my bergs to dare,
Ye have but my drifts to conquer. Go forth, for it is there!"

The South Wind sighed:—"From The Virgins my mid-sea
    course was ta'en
Over a thousand islands lost in an idle main,
Where the sea-egg flames on the coral and the long-backed
    breakers croon
Their endless ocean legends to the lazy, locked lagoon.

"Strayed amid lonely islets, mazed amid outer keys,
I waked the palms to laughter—I tossed the scud in the
    breeze—
Never was isle so little, never was sea so lone,
But over the scud and the palm-trees an English flag was
    flown.

"I have wrenched it free from the halliard, to hang for a wisp
    on the Horn;
I have chased it north to the Lizard—ribboned and rolled
    and torn;

I have spread its fold o'er the dying, adrift in a hopeless sea;
I have hurled it swift on the slaver, and seen the slaves set
   free.

"My basking sunfish know it, and wheeling albatross,
Where the lone wave fills with fire beneath the Southern
   Cross.
What is the Flag of England? Ye have but my reefs to dare,
Ye have but my seas to furrow. Go forth, for it is there!"

The East Wind roared:—"From the Kuriles, the Bitter Seas,
   I come,
And me men call the Home-Wind, for I bring the English
   home.
Look—look well to your shipping! By the breath of my
   mad typhoon
I swept your close-packed Praya and beached your best at
   Kowloon!

"The reeling junks behind me and the racing seas before,
I raped your richest roadstead—I plundered Singapore!
I set my hand on the Hoogli; as a hooded snake she rose,
And I flung your stoutest steamers to roost with the startled
   crows.

"Never the lotos closes, never the wild-fowl wake,
But a soul goes out on the East Wind that died for England's
   sake—
Man or woman or suckling, mother or bride or maid—
Because on the bones of the English the English Flag is
   stayed.

"The desert-dust hath dimmed it, the flying wild-ass knows.
The scared white leopard winds it across the taintless snows.
What is the Flag of England? Ye have but my sun to dare,
Ye have but my sands to travel. Go forth, for it is there!"

The West Wind called:—"In squadrons the thoughtless gal-
    leons fly
That bear the wheat and cattle lest street-bred people die.
They make my might their porter, they make my house their
    path,
Till I loose my neck from their rudder and whelm them all
    in my wrath.

"I draw the gliding fog-bank as a snake is drawn from the
    hole;
They bellow one to the other, the frightened ship-bells toll,
For day is a drifting terror till I raise the shroud with my
    breath,
And they see strange bows above them and the two go
    locked to death.

"But whether in calm or wrack-wreath, whether by dark or
    day,
I heave them whole to the conger or rip their plates away,
First of the scattered legions, under a shrieking sky,
Dipping between the rollers, the English Flag goes by.

"The dead dumb fog hath wrapped it—the frozen dews
    have kissed—
The naked stars have seen it, a fellow-star in the mist.
What is the Flag of England? Ye have but my breath to
    dare,
Ye have but my waves to conquer. Go forth, for it is there!"

XXV

TO THE UNKNOWN GODDESS

From *Departmental Ditties and Ballads and Barrack-Room Ballads*

WILL you conquer my heart with your beauty, my soul
going out from afar?
Shall I fall to your hand as a victim of crafty and cautious
shikar?

Have I met you and passed you already, unknowing, un-
thinking, and blind?
Shall I meet you next session at Simla, oh, sweetest and best
of your kind?

     .   .   .   .

Ah, Goddess! child, spinster, or widow—as of old on Mars
Hill when they raised
To the God that they knew not an altar—so I, a young
Pagan, have praised

The Goddess I know not nor worship; yet, if half that men
tell me be true,
You will come in the future, and therefore these verses are
written to you.

XXVI

THE GALLEY SLAVE

From *Departmental Ditties and Ballads and Barrack-Room Ballads*

O H, GALLANT was our galley from her carven steering-
 wheel
To her figurehead of silver and her beak of hammered steel;
The leg-bar chafed the ankle, and we gasped for cooler air,
But no galley on the water with our galley could compare!

Our bulkheads bulged with cotton and our masts were
 stepped in gold—
We ran a mighty merchandise of Negroes in the hold;
The white foam spun behind us, and the black shark swam
 below,
As we gripped the kicking sweep-head and we made that
 galley go.

It was merry in the galley, for we revelled now and then—
If they wore us down like cattle, faith, we fought and loved
 like men!
As we snatched her through the water, so we snatched a
 minute's bliss,
And the mutter of the dying never spoiled the lover's kiss.

Our women and our children toiled beside us in the dark—
They died, we filed their fetters, and we heaved them to the
    shark—
We heaved them to the fishes, but so fast the galley sped,
We had only time to envy, for we could not mourn our
    dead.

Bear witness, once my comrades, what a hard-bit gang were
    we—
The servants of the sweep-head, but the masters of the sea!
By the hands that drove her forward as she plunged and
    yawed and sheered,
Woman, Man, or God, or Devil, was there anything we
    feared?

Was it storm? Our fathers faced it, and a wilder never blew;
Earth that waited for the wreckage watched the galley
    struggle through.
Burning noon or choking midnight, Sickness, Sorrow, Part-
    ing, Death?
Nay our very babes would mock you, had they time for idle
    breath.

But to-day I leave the galley, and another takes my place;
There's my name upon the deck-beam—let it stand a little
    space.
I am free—to watch my messmates beating out to open
    main,
Free of all that Life can offer—save to handle sweep again.

By the brand upon my shoulder, by the gall of clinging steel,
By the welt the whips have left me, by the scars that never
    heal;

By eyes grown old with staring through the sun-wash on the
brine,
I am paid in full for service—would that service still were
mine!

. . . .

It may be that Fate will give me life and leave to row once
more—
Set some strong man free for fighting as I take awhile his
oar.
But to-day I leave the galley. Shall I curse her service then?
God be thanked—whate'er comes after, I have lived and
toiled with men!

XXVII

THE SHIP THAT FOUND HERSELF

From *The Day's Work*

IT WAS her first voyage, and though she was but a cargo-steamer of twenty-five hundred tons, she was the very best of her kind, the outcome of forty years of experiments and improvements in framework and machinery; and her designers and owner thought as much of her as though she had been the *Lucania*. Anyone can make a floating hotel that will pay expenses, if he puts enough money into the saloon, and charges for private baths, suites of rooms, and such like; but in these days of competition and low freights every square inch of a cargo-boat must be built for cheapness, great hold-capacity, and a certain steady speed. This boat was, perhaps, two hundred and forty feet long and thirty-two feet wide, with arrangements that enabled her to carry cattle on her main and sheep on her upper deck if she wanted to; but her great glory was the amount of cargo that she could store away in her holds. Her owners—they were a very well-known Scotch firm—came round with her from the north, where she had been launched and christened and fitted, to Liverpool, where she was to take cargo for New York; and the owner's daughter, Miss Frazier, went to and fro on the clean decks, admiring the new paint and the brass work, and the patent winches, and particularly the strong, straight bow, over which she had cracked a bottle of champagne when she named the steamer the *Dimbula.* It was a beautiful September afternoon, and the boat in all her newness—she was painted lead-colour with a red funnel—looked very fine indeed. Her house-flag was flying, and her whistle from time to time acknowledged the salutes of friendly boats, who saw that she was new to the High and Narrow Seas and wished to make her welcome.

"And now," said Miss Frazier, delightedly, to the captain, "she's a real ship, is n't she? It seems only the other day father gave the order for her, and now—and now—is n't she a beauty!" The girl was proud of the firm, and talked as though she were the controlling partner.

"Oh, she's no so bad," the skipper replied cautiously. "But I 'm sayin' that it takes more than christenin' to mak' a ship. In the nature o' things, Miss Frazier, if ye follow me, she's just irons and rivets and plates put into the form of a ship. She has to find herself yet."

"I thought father said she was exceptionally well found."

"So she is," said the skipper, with a laugh. "But it 's this way wi' ships, Miss Frazier. She's all here, but the parrts of her have not learned to work together yet. They 've had no chance."

"The engines are working beautifully. I can hear them."

"Yes, indeed. But there 's more than engines to a ship. Every inch of her, ye 'll understand, has to be livened up and made to work wi' its neighbour—sweetenin' her, we call it, technically."

"And how will you do it?" the girl asked.

"We can no more than drive and steer her, and so forth; but if we have rough weather this trip—it 's likely—she 'll learn the rest by heart! For a ship, ye 'll obsairve, Miss Frazier, is in no sense a reegid body closed at both ends. She 's a highly complex structure o' various an' conflictin' strains, wi' tissues that must give an' tak' accordin' to her personal modulus of elasteecity." Mr. Buchanan, the chief engineer, was coming toward them. "I 'm sayin' to Miss Frazier, here, that our little *Dimbula* has to be sweetened yet, and nothin' but a gale will do it. How 's all wi' your engines, Buck?"

"Well enough—true by plumb an' rule, o' course; but there 's no spontaneeity yet." He turned to the girl. "Take my word, Miss Frazier, and maybe ye 'll comprehend later; even after a pretty girl's christened a ship it does not follow that there 's such a thing as a ship under the men that work her."

"I was sayin' the very same, Mr. Buchanan," the skipper interrupted.

"That 's more metaphysical than I can follow," said Miss Frazier, laughing.

"Why so? Ye 're good Scotch, an'—I knew your mother's father, he was fra' Dumfries—ye 've a vested right in metapheesics, Miss Frazier, just as ye have in the *Dimbula*," the engineer said.

"Eh, well, we must go down to the deep watters, an' earn Miss Frazier her deevidends. Will you not come to my cabin for tea?" said the skipper. "We 'll be in dock the night, and when you 're goin' back to Glasgie ye can think of us loadin' her down an' drivin' her forth—all for your sake."

In the next few days they stowed some four thousand tons' dead weight into the *Dimbula,* and took her out from Liverpool. As soon as she met the lift of the open water, she naturally began to talk. If you lay your ear to the side of the cabin next time you are in a steamer, you will hear hundreds of little voices in every direction, thrilling and buzzing, and whispering and popping, and gurgling and sobbing and squeaking exactly like a telephone in a thunder-storm. Wooden ships shriek and growl and grunt, but iron vessels throb and quiver through all their hundreds of ribs and thousands of rivets. The *Dimbula* was very strongly built, and every piece of her had a letter or number, or both, to describe it; and every piece had been hammered, or forged, or rolled, or punched by man, and had lived in the roar and rattle of the shipyard for months. Therefore, every piece had its own separate voice in exact proportion to the amount of trouble spent upon it. Cast-iron as a rule, says very little; but mild steel plates and wrought-iron, and ribs and beams that have been much bent and welded and riveted, talk continuously. Their conversation, of course, is not half as wise as our human talk, because they are all, though they do not know it, bound down one to the other in a black darkness, where they cannot tell what is happening near them, nor what will overtake them next.

As soon as she had cleared the Irish coast a sullen gray-headed old wave of the Atlantic climbed leisurely over her straight bows, and sat down on her steam-capstan used for hauling up the anchor. Now the capstan and the engine that drove it had been newly painted red and green; besides which, nobody likes being ducked.

"Don't you do that again," the capstan sputtered through the teeth of his cogs. "Hi! Where 's the fellow gone?"

The wave had slouched overside with a plop and a chuckle; but "Plenty more where he came from," said a brother-wave, and went through and over the capstan, who was bolted firmly to an iron plate on the iron deck-beams below.

"Can't you keep still up there?" said the deck-beams.

"What 's the matter with you? One minute you weigh twice as much as you ought to, and the next you don't!"

"It is n't my fault," said the capstan. "There 's a green brute outside that comes and hits me on the head."

"Tell that to the shipwrights. You 've been in position for months and you 've never wriggled like this before. If you are n't careful you 'll strain *us*."

"Talking of strain," said a low, rasping, unpleasant voice, "are any of you fellows—you deck-beams, we mean—aware that those exceedingly ugly knees of yours happen to be riveted into our structure—*ours?*"

"Who might you be?" the deck-beams inquired.

"Oh, nobody in particular," was the answer. "We 're only the port and starboard upper-deck stringers; and if you persist in heaving and hiking like this, we shall be reluctantly compelled to take steps."

Now the stringers of the ship are long iron girders, so to speak, that run lengthways from stern to bow. They keep the iron frames (what are called ribs in a wooden ship) in place, and also help to hold the ends of the deck-beams, which go from side to side of the ship. Stringers always consider themselves most important, because they are so long.

"You will take steps—will you?" This was a long echoing rumble. It came from the frames—scores and scores of them, each one about eighteen inches distant from the next, and each riveted to the stringers in four places. "We think you will have a certain amount of trouble in *that;*" and thousands and thousands of the little rivets that held everything together whispered: "You will. You will! Stop quivering and be quiet. Hold on, brethren! Hold on! Hot Punches! What 's that?"

Rivets have no teeth, so they cannot chatter with fright;

but they did their best as a fluttering jar swept along the ship from stern to bow, and she shook like a rat in a terrier's mouth.

An unusually severe pitch, for the sea was rising, had lifted the big throbbing screw nearly to the surface, and it was spinning round in a kind of soda-water—half sea and half air—going much faster than was proper, because there was no deep water for it to work in. As it sank again, the engines —and they were triple expansion, three cylinders in a row— snorted through all their three pistons, "Was that a joke, you fellow outside? It's an uncommonly poor one. How are we to do our work if you fly off the handle that way?"

"I did n't fly off the handle," said the screw, twirling huskily at the end of the screw-shaft. "If I had, you 'd have been scrap-iron by this time. The sea dropped away from under me, and I had nothing to catch on to. That 's all."

"That 's all, d 'you call it?" said the thrust-block whose business it is to take the push of the screw; for if a screw had nothing to hold it back it would crawl right into the engine-room. (It is the holding back of the screwing action that gives the drive to a ship.) "I know I do my work deep down and out of sight, but I warn you I expect justice. All I ask for is bare justice. Why can't you push steadily and evenly instead of whizzing like a whirligig, and making me hot under all my collars." The thrust-block had six collars, each faced with brass, and he did not wish to get them heated.

All the bearings that supported the fifty feet of screw-shaft as it ran to the stern whispered: "Justice—give us justice."

"I can only give you what I can get," the screw answered. "Look out! It 's coming again!"

He rose with a roar as the *Dimbula* plunged, and "whack —flack—whack—whack" went the engines, furiously, for they had little to check them.

"I'm the noblest outcome of human ingenuity—Mr. Buchanan says so," squealed the high-pressure cylinder. "This is simply ridiculous!" The piston went up savagely, and choked, for half the steam behind it was mixed with dirty water. "Help! Oiler! Fitter! Stoker! Help! I'm choking," it gasped. "Never in the history of maritime invention has such a calamity overtaken one so young and strong. And if I go, who's to drive the ship?"

"Hush! oh, hush!" whispered the Steam, who, of course, had been to sea many times before. He used to spend his leisure ashore in a cloud, or a gutter, or a flower-pot, or a thunder-storm, or anywhere else where water was needed. "That's only a little priming, a little carrying-over, as they call it. It'll happen all night, on and off. I don't say it's nice, but it's the best we can do under the circumstances."

"What difference can circumstances make? I'm here to do my work—on clean, dry steam. Blow circumstances!" the cylinder roared.

"The circumstances will attend to the blowing. I've worked on the North Atlantic run a good many times—it's going to be rough before morning."

"It isn't distressingly calm now," said the extra-strong frames—they were called web-frames—in the engine-room. "There's an upward thrust that we don't understand, and there's a twist that's very bad for our brackets and diamond-plates, and there's a sort of west-north-westerly pull that follows the twist, which seriously annoys us. We mention this because we happened to cost a good deal of money, and we feel sure that the owner would not approve of our being treated in this frivolous way."

"I'm afraid the matter is out of owner's hands for the present," said the Steam, slipping into the condenser. "You're left to your own devices till the weather betters."

"I wouldn't mind the weather," said a flat bass voice below; "it's this confounded cargo that's breaking my heart. I'm the garboard-strake, and I'm twice as thick as most of the others, and I ought to know something."

The garboard-strake is the lowest plate in the bottom of a ship, and the *Dimbula's* garboard-strake was nearly three-quarters of an inch mild steel.

"The sea pushes me up in a way I should never have expected," the strake grunted, "and the cargo pushes me down, and, between the two, I don't know what I'm supposed to do."

"When in doubt, hold on," rumbled the Steam, making head in the boilers.

"Yes; but there's only dark, and cold, and hurry, down here; and how do I know whether the other plates are doing their duty? Those bulwark-plates up above, I've heard, ain't more than five-sixteenths of an inch thick—scandalous, I call it."

"I agree with you," said a huge web-frame by the main cargo-hatch. He was deeper and thicker than all the others, and curved half-way across the ship in the shape of half an arch, to support the deck where deck beams would have been in the way of cargo coming up and down. "I work entirely unsupported, and I observe that I am the sole strength of this vessel, so far as my vision extends. The responsibility, I assure you, is enormous. I believe the money-value of the cargo is over one hundred and fifty thousand pounds. Think of that!"

"And every pound of it is dependent on my personal exertions." Here spoke a sea-valve that communicated directly with the water outside, and was seated not very far from the garboard-strake. "I rejoice to think that I am a Prince-Hyde Valve, with best Para rubber facings. Five patents cover me—I mention this without pride—five separate and several patents, each one finer than the other. At present I am screwed fast. Should I open, you would immediately be swamped. This is incontrovertible!"

Patent things always use the longest words they can. It is a trick that they pick up from their inventors.

"That 's news," said a big centrifugal bilge-pump. "I had an idea that you were employed to clean decks and things with. At least, I 've used you for that more than once. I forget the precise number, in thousands, of gallons which I am guaranteed to throw per hour; but I assure you, my complaining friends, that there is not the least danger. I alone am capable of clearing any water that may find its way here. By my Biggest Deliveries, we pitched then!"

The sea was getting up in workmanlike style. It was a dead westerly gale, blown from under a ragged opening of green sky, narrowed on all sides by fat, gray clouds; and the wind bit like pincers as it fretted the spray into lacework on the flanks of the waves.

"I tell you what it is," the foremast telephoned down its wire-stays. "I 'm up here, and I can take a dispassionate view of things. There 's an organized conspiracy against us. I 'm sure of it, because every single one of these waves is heading directly for our bows. The whole sea is concerned in it—and so 's the wind. It 's awful!"

"What 's awful?" said a wave, drowning the capstan for the hundredth time.

"This organized conspiracy on your part," the capstan gurgled, taking his cue from the mast.

"Organized bubbles and spindrift! There has been a de-

pression in the Gulf of Mexico. Excuse me!" He leaped overside; but his friends took up the tale one after another.

"Which has advanced——" That wave hove green water
over the funnel.

"As far as Cape Hatteras——" He drenched the bridge.

"And is now going out to sea—to sea—to sea!" The third
went free in three surges, making a clean sweep of a boat,
which turned bottom up and sank in the darkening troughs
alongside, while the broken falls whipped the davits.

"That's all there is to it," seethed the white water roaring
through the scuppers. "There's no animus in our proceed-
ings. We're only meteorological corollaries."

"Is it going to get any worse?" said the bow-anchor,
chained down to the deck, where he could only breathe once
in five minutes.

"Not knowing, can't say. Wind may blow a bit by midnight. Thanks awfully. Good-bye."

The wave that spoke so politely had travelled some distance aft, and found itself all mixed up on the deck
amidships, which was a well-deck sunk between high bul-
warks. One of the bulwark plates, which was hung on hinges
to open outward, had swung out, and passed the bulk of the
water back to the sea again with a clean smack.

"Evidently that's what I'm made for," said the plate, clos-
ing again with a sputter of pride. "Oh, no, you don't, my
friend!"

The top of a wave was trying to get in from the outside,
but as the plate did not open in that direction, the defeated
water spurted back.

"Not bad for five-sixteenths of an inch," said the bulwark-
plate. "My work, I see, is laid down for the night"; and it
began opening and shutting, as it was designed to do, with
the motion of the ship.

"We are not what you might call idle," groaned all the frames together, as the *Dimbula* climbed a big wave, lay on her side at the top, and shot into the next hollow, twisting in the descent. A huge swell pushed up exactly under her middle, and her bow and stern hung free with nothing to support them. Then one joking wave caught her up at the bow, and another at the stern, while the rest of the water slunk away from under her just to see how she would like it; so she was held up at her two ends only, and the weight of the cargo and the machinery fell on the groaning iron keels and bilge-stringers.

"Ease off! Ease off, there!" roared the garboard-strake. "I want one-eighth of an inch fair play. D' you hear me, you rivets!"

"Ease off! Ease off!" cried the bilge-stringers. "Don't hold us so tight to the frames!"

"Ease off!" grunted the deck-beams, as the *Dimbula* rolled fearfully. "You 've cramped our knees into the stringers, and we can't move. Ease off, you flat-headed little nuisances."

Then two converging seas hit the bows, one on each side, and fell away in torrents of streaming thunder.

"Ease off!" shouted the forward collision-bulkhead. "I want to crumple up, but I 'm stiffened in every direction. Ease off, you dirty little forge-filings. Let me breathe!"

All the hundreds of plates that are riveted to the frames, and make the outside skin of every steamer, echoed the call, for each plate wanted to shift and creep a little, and each plate, according to its position, complained against the rivets.

"We can't help it! *We* can't help it!" they murmured in reply. "We 're put here to hold you, and we 're going to do it; you never pull us twice in the same direction. If you 'd say what you were going to do next, we 'd try to meet your views."

"As far as I could feel," said the upper-deck planking, and that was four inches thick, "every single iron near me was pushing or pulling in opposite directions. Now, what 's the sense of that? My friends, let us all pull together."

"Pull any way you please," roared the funnel, "so long as you don't try your experiments on *me*. I need fourteen wire ropes, all pulling in different directions, to hold me steady. Is n't that so?"

"We believe you, my boy!" whistled the funnel-stays through their clinched teeth, as they twanged in the wind from the top of the funnel to the deck.

"Nonsense! We must all pull together," the decks repeated. "Pull lengthways."

"Very good," said the stringers; "then stop pushing sideways when you get wet. Be content to run gracefully fore and aft, and curve in at the ends as we do."

"No—no curves at the end! A very slight workmanlike curve from side to side, with a good grip at each knee, and little pieces welded on," said the deck-beams.

"Fiddle!" cried the iron pillars of the deep, dark hold. "Who ever heard of curves? Stand up straight; be a perfectly round column, and carry tons of good solid weight—like that! There!" A big sea smashed on the deck above, and the pillars stiffened themselves to the load.

"Straight up and down is not bad," said the frames, who ran that way in the sides of the ship, "but you must also expand yourselves sideways. Expansion is the law of life, children. Open out! open out!"

"Come back!" said the deck-beams, savagely, as the upward heave of the sea made the frames try to open. "Come back to your bearings, you slack-jawed irons!"

"Rigidity! Rigidity! Rigidity!" thumped the engines. "Absolute, unvarying rigidity—rigidity!"

"You see!" whined the rivets, in chorus. "No two of you will ever pull alike, and—and you blame it all on us. We only know how to go through a plate and bite down on both sides so that it can't, and must n't, and shan't move."

"I 've got one-fraction of an inch play, at any rate," said the garboard-strake, triumphantly. So he had, and all the bottom of the ship felt the easier for it.

"Then we 're no good," sobbed the bottom rivets. "We were ordered—we were ordered—never to give; and we 've given, and the sea will come in, and we 'll all go to the bottom together! First we 're blamed for everything unpleasant, and now we have n't the consolation of having done our work."

"Don't say I told you," whispered the Steam, consolingly; but, between you and me and the last cloud I came from, it was bound to happen sooner or later. You *had* to give a fraction, and you 've given without knowing it. Now, hold on, as before."

"What 's the use?" a few hundred rivets chattered. "We 've given—we 've given; and the sooner we confess that we can't keep the ship together, and go off our little heads, the easier it will be. No rivet forged can stand this strain."

"No one rivet was ever meant to. Share it among you," the Steam answered.

"The others can have my share. I 'm going to pull out," said a rivet in one of the forward plates.

"If you go, others will follow," hissed the Steam. "There 's nothing so contagious in a boat as rivets going. Why, I knew a little chap like you—he was an eighth of an inch fatter, though—on a steamer—to be sure, she was only twelve hundred tons, now I come to think of it—in exactly the same place as you are. He pulled out in a bit of a bobble of a sea, not half as bad as this, and he started all his friends on the same butt-strap, and the plates opened like a furnace door, and I had to climb into the nearest fog-bank, while the boat went down."

"Now that 's peculiarly disgraceful," said the rivet. "Fatter than me, was he, and in a steamer not half our tonnage? Reedy little peg! I blush for the family, sir." He settled himself more firmly than ever in his place, and the Steam chuckled.

"You see," he went on, quite gravely, "a rivet, and especially a rivet in your position, is really the one indispensable part of the ship."

The Steam did not say that he had whispered the very same thing to every single piece of iron aboard. There is no sense in telling too much truth.

And all that while the little *Dimbula* pitched and chopped, and swung and slewed, and lay down as though she were going to die, and got up as though she had been stung, and threw her nose round and round in circles half a dozen times as she dipped; for the gale was at its worst. It was inky black, in spite of the tearing white froth on the waves, and, to top everything, the rain began to fall in sheets, so that you could not see your hand before your face. This did not make much difference to the ironwork below, but it troubled the foremast a good deal.

"Now it 's all finished," he said dismally. "The conspiracy is too strong for us. There is nothing left but to——"

"*Hurraar! Brrrraaah! Brrrrrrp!*" roared the Steam through the fog-horn, till the decks quivered. "Don't be frightened, below. It 's only me, just throwing out a few words, in case any one happens to be rolling round to-night."

"You don't mean to say there 's any one except *us* on the sea in such weather?" said the funnel in a husky snuffle.

"Scores of 'em," said the Steam, clearing its throat; "*Rrrrrraaa! Brraaaaa! Prrrrp!* It's a trifle windy up here; and, Great Boilers! how it rains!"

"We're drowning," said the scuppers. They had been doing nothing else all night, but this steady thrash of rain above them seemed to be the end of the world.

"That's all right. We'll be easier in an hour or two. First the wind and then the rain: Soon you may make sail again! *Grrraaaaaah! Drrrraaaa! Drrrp!* I have a notion that the sea is going down already. If it does you'll learn something about rolling. We've only pitched till now. By the way, are n't you chaps in the hold a little easier than you were?"

There was just as much groaning and straining as ever, but it was not so loud or squeaky in tone; and when the ship quivered she did not jar stiffly, like a poker hit on the floor, but gave with a supple little waggle, like a perfectly balanced golf-club.

"We have made a most amazing discovery," said the stringers, one after another. "A discovery that entirely changes the situation. We have found, for the first time in the history of ship-building, that the inward pull of the deck-beams and the outward thrust of the frames locks us, as it were, more closely in our places, and enables us to endure a strain which is entirely without parallel in the records of marine architecture."

The Steam turned a laugh quickly into a roar up the fog-horn. "What massive intellects you great stringers have," he said softly, when he had finished.

"We also," began the deck-beams, "are discoverers and geniuses. We are of opinion that the support of the hold-pillars materially helps us. We find that we lock up on them when we are subjected to a heavy and singular weight of sea above."

Here the *Dimbula* shot down a hollow, lying almost on her side—righting at the bottom with a wrench and a spasm.

"In these cases—are you aware of this, Steam?—the plating at the bows, and particularly at the stern—we would also mention the floors beneath us—help *us* to resist any tendency to spring." The frames spoke, in the solemn, awed voice which people use when they have just come across something entirely new for the very first time.

"I'm only a poor puffy little flutterer," said the Steam, "but I have to stand a good deal of pressure in my business. It's all tremendously interesting. Tell us some more. You fellows are so strong."

"Watch us and you'll see," said the bow-plates, proudly. "Ready, behind there! Here's the Father and Mother of Waves coming! Sit tight, rivets all!" A great sluicing comber thundered by, but through the scuffle and confusion the Steam could hear the low, quick cries of the ironwork as the various strains took them—cries like these: "Easy, now—easy! *Now* push for all your strength! Hold out! Give a fraction! Hold up! Pull in! Shove crossways! Mind the strain at the ends! Grip, now! Bite tight! Let the water get away from under—and there she goes!"

The wave raced off into the darkness, shouting, "Not bad, that, if it's your first run!" and the drenched and ducked ship throbbed to the beat of the engines inside her. All three cylinders were white with the salt spray that had come down through the engine-room hatch; there was white fur on the canvas-bound steam-pipes, and even the bright-work deep below was speckled and soiled; but the cylinders had learned to make the most of steam that was half water, and were pounding along cheerfully.

"How's the noblest outcome of human ingenuity hitting it?" said the Steam, as he whirled through the engine-room.

"Nothing for nothing in this world of woe," the cylinders answered, as though they had been working for centuries, "and precious little for seventy-five pounds' head. We 've made two knots this last hour and a quarter! Rather humiliating for eight hundred horse-power, is n't it?"

"Well, it 's better than drifting astern, at any rate. You seem rather less—how shall I put it?—stiff in the back than you were."

"If you 'd been hammered as we 've been this night, you would n't be stiff—iff—iff, either. Theoreti—retti—retti—cally, of course, rigidity is the thing. Purrr—purr—practically, there has to be a little give and take. We found that out by working on our sides for five minutes at a stretch—chch—chh. How 's the weather?"

"Sea 's going down fast," said the Steam.

"Good business," said the high-pressure cylinder. "Whack her up, boys. They 've given us five pounds more steam"; and he began humming the first bars of "Said the Young Obadiah to the Old Obadiah," which, as you may have noticed, is a pet tune among engines not built for high speed. Racing-liners with twin-screws sing "The Turkish Patrol" and the overture to the "Bronze Horse," and "Madame Angot," till something goes wrong, and then they render Gounod's "Funeral March of a Marionette" with variations.

"You 'll learn a song of your own some fine day," said the Steam, as he flew up the fog-horn for one last bellow.

Next day the sky cleared and the sea dropped a little, and the *Dimbula* began to roll from side to side till every inch of iron in her was sick and giddy. But luckily they did not all feel ill at the same time: otherwise she would have opened out like a wet paper box.

The Steam whistled warnings as he went about his business: it is in this short, quick roll and tumble that follows a heavy sea that most of the accidents happen, for then every-thing thinks that the worst is over and goes off guard. So he orated and chattered till the beams and frames and floors and stringers and things had learned how to lock down and lock up on one another, and endure this new kind of strain.

They found ample time to practise, for they were sixteen days at sea, and it was foul weather till within a hundred miles of New York. The *Dimbula* picked up her pilot and came in covered with salt and red rust. Her funnel was dirty gray from top to bottom; two boats had been carried away; three copper ventilators looked like hats after a fight with the police; the bridge had a dimple in the middle of it; the house that covered the steam steering-gear was split as with hatchets; there was a bill for small repairs in the engine-room almost as long as the screw-shaft; the forward cargo-hatch fell into bucket-staves when they raised the iron cross-bars; and the steam-capstan had been badly wrenched on its bed. Altogether, as the skipper said, it was "a pretty general average."

"But she 's soupled," he said to Mr. Buchanan. "For all her dead weight she rode like a yacht. Ye mind that last blow off the Banks? I am proud of her, Buck."

"It 's vera good," said the chief engineer, looking along the dishevelled decks. "Now, a man judgin' superfeecially would say we were a wreck, but we know otherwise—by experience."

Naturally everything in the *Dimbula* fairly stiffened with pride, and the foremast and the forward collision-bulkhead who are pushing creatures, begged the Steam to warn the Port of New York of their arrival. "Tell those big boats all about us," they said. "They seem to take us quite as a matter of course."

It was a glorious, clear, dead calm morning, and in single file, with less than half a mile between each, their bands playing and their tugboats shouting and waving handkerchiefs, were the *Majestic,* the *Paris,* the *Touraine,* the *Servia,* the *Kaiser Wilhelm II.,* and the *Werkendam,* all statelily going out to sea. As the *Dimbula* shifted her helm to give the great boats clear way, the Steam (who knows far too much to mind making an exhibition of himself now and then) shouted:

"Oyez! Oyez! Oyez! Princes, Dukes, and Barons of the High Seas! Know ye by these presents, we are the *Dimbula,* fifteen days nine hours from Liverpool, having crossed the Atlantic with four thousand ton of cargo for the first time in our career! We have not foundered. We are here. 'Eer! 'Eer! We are not disabled. But we have had a time wholly unparalleled in the annals of ship-building! Our decks were swept! We pitched; we rolled! We thought we were going to die! *Hi! Hi!* But we did n't. We wish to give notice that we have come to New York all the way across the Atlantic through the worst weather in the world; and we are the *Dimbula!* We are—arr—ha—ha—ha-r-r-r!"

The beautiful line of boats swept by as steadily as the procession of the Seasons. The *Dimbula* heard the *Majestic* say, "Hmph!" and the *Paris* grunted, "How!" and the *Touraine* said, "Oui!" with a little coquettish flicker of steam; and the *Servia* said, "Haw!" and the *Kaiser* and the *Werkendam* said, "Hoch!" Dutch fashion—and that was absolutely all.

"I did my best," said the Steam, gravely, "but I don't think they were much impressed with us, somehow. Do you?"

"It 's simply disgusting," said the bow-plates. "They might have seen what we 've been through. There is n't a ship on the sea that has suffered as we have—is there, now?"

"Well, I would n't go so far as that," said the Steam, "because I 've worked on some of those boats, and sent them through weather quite as bad as the fortnight that we 've had, in six days; and some of them are a little over ten thousand tons, I believe. Now I 've seen the *Majestic*, for instance, ducked from her bows to her funnel; and I 've helped the *Arizona*, I think she was, to back off an iceberg she met with one dark night; and I had to run out of the *Paris's* engine-room, one day, because there was thirty foot of water in it. Of course, I don't deny——" The Steam shut off suddenly, as a tug-boat, loaded with a political club and a brass band, that had been to see a New York Senator off to Europe, crossed their bows, going to Hoboken. There was a long silence that reached, without a break, from the cut-water to the propeller-blades of the *Dimbula*.

Then a new, big voice said slowly and thickly, as though the owner had just waked up: "It 's my conviction that I have made a fool of myself."

The Steam knew what had happened at once, for when a ship finds herself all the talking of the separate pieces ceases and melts into one voice, which is the soul of the ship.

"Who are you?" he said, with a laugh.

"I am the *Dimbula*, of course. I 've never been anything else except that—and a fool!"

The tugboat, which was doing its very best to be run down, got away just in time, its band playing clashily and brassily a popular but impolite air:

> In the days of old Rameses—are you on?
> In the days of old Rameses—are you on?
> In the days of old Rameses,
> That story had paresis,
> Are you on—are you on—are you on?

"Well, I'm glad you've found yourself," said the Steam. "To tell the truth I was a little tired of talking to all those ribs and stringers. Here's Quarantine. After that we'll go to our wharf and clean up a little, and—next month we'll do it all over again."

XXVIII

A TRIP ACROSS A CONTINENT

From *Captains Courageous*

CHEYNE was flying to meet the only son, so miraculously restored to him. The bear was seeking his cub, not the bulls. Hard men who had their knives drawn to fight for their financial lives put away the weapons and wished him God-speed, while half a dozen panic-smitten tin-pot roads perked up their heads and spoke of the wonderful things they would have done had not Cheyne buried the hatchet.

It was a busy week-end among the wires; for, now that their anxiety was removed, men and cities hastened to accommodate. Los Angeles called to San Diego and Barstow that the Southern California engineers might know and be ready in their lonely roundhouses; Barstow passed the word to the Atlantic and Pacific; and Albuquerque flung it the whole length of the Atchison, Topeka, and Santa Fé management, even into Chicago. An engine, combination-car with crew, and the great and gilded "Constance" private car were to be "expedited" over those two thousand three hundred and fifty miles. The train would take precedence of one hundred and seventy-seven others meeting and passing; despatchers and crews of every one of those said trains must be notified. Sixteen locomotives; sixteen engineers, and sixteen firemen would be needed—each and every one the best available. Two and one-half minutes would be allowed for changing engines, three for watering, and two for coaling. "Warn the men, and arrange tanks and chutes accordingly; for Harvey Cheyne is in a hurry, a hurry—hurry," sang the wires. "Forty miles an hour will be expected, and division superintendents will accompany this special over their respective divisions. From San Diego to Sixteenth Street, Chicago, let the magic carpet be laid down. Hurry! oh, hurry!"

"It will be hot," said Cheyne, as they rolled out of San Diego in the dawn of Sunday. "We 're going to hurry, mamma, just as fast as ever we can; but I really don't think there 's any good of your putting on your bonnet and gloves yet. You 'd much better lie down and take your medicine. I 'd play you a game o' dominoes, but it 's Sunday."

"I 'll be good. Oh, I *will* be good. Only—taking off my bonnet makes me feel as if we 'd never get there."

"Try to sleep a little, mamma, and we 'll be in Chicago before you know."

"But it 's Boston, father. Tell them to hurry."

The six-foot drivers were hammering their way to San Bernardino and the Mohave wastes, but this was no grade for speed. That would come later. The heat of the desert followed the heat of the hills as they turned east to the Needles and the Colorado River. The car cracked in the utter drought and glare, and they put crushed ice to Mrs. Cheyne's neck, and toiled up the long, long grades, past Ash Fork, toward Flagstaff, where the forests and quarries are, under the dry, remote skies. The needle of the speed-indicator flicked and wagged to and fro, the cinders rattled on the roof, and a whirl of dust sucked after the whirling wheels. The crew of the combination sat on their bunks, panting in their shirt-sleeves, and Cheyne found himself among them shouting old, old stories of the railroad that every trainman knows, above the roar of the car. He told them about his son, and how the sea had given up its dead, and they nodded and spat and rejoiced with him; asked after "her, back there," and whether she could stand it if the engineer "let her out a piece," and Cheyne thought she could. Accordingly the great fire-horse was "led out" from Flagstaff to Winslow, till a division superintendent protested.

But Mrs. Cheyne, in the boudoir stateroom, where the French maid, sallow-white with fear, clung to the silver door-handle, only moaned a little and begged her husband to bid them "hurry." And so they dropped the dry sands and moon-struck rocks of Arizona behind them, and grilled on till the crash of the couplings and the wheeze of the brake-hose told them they were at Coolidge by the Continental Divide.

Three bold and experienced men—cool, confident, and dry when they began; white, quivering, and wet when they finished their trick at those terrible wheels—swung her over the great lift from Albuquerque to Glorietta and beyond Springer, up and up to the Raton Tunnel on the State line, whence they dropped rocking into La Junta, had sight of the Arkansaw, and tore down the long slope to Dodge City, where Cheyne took comfort once again from setting his watch an hour ahead.

There was very little talk in the car. The secretary and typewriter sat together on the stamped Spanish-leather cushions by the plate-glass observation-window at the rear end, watching the surge and ripple of the ties crowded back behind them, and, it is believed, making notes of the scenery. Cheyne moved nervously between his own extravagant gorgeousness and the naked necessity of the combination, an unlit cigar in his teeth, till the pitying crews forgot that he was their tribal enemy, and did their best to entertain him.

At night the bunched electrics lit up that distressful palace of all the luxuries, and they fared sumptuously, swinging on through the emptiness of abject desolation. Now they heard the swish of a water-tank, and the guttural voice of a Chinaman, the clink-clink of hammers that tested the Krupp steel wheels, and the oath of a tramp chased off the rear-platform; now the solid crash of coal shot into the tender; and now a beating back of noises as they flew past a waiting train. Now they looked out into great abysses, a trestle purring beneath their tread, or up to rocks that barred out half the stars. Now scaur and ravine changed and rolled back to jagged mountains on the horizon's edge, and now broke into hills lower and lower, till at last came the true plains.

At Dodge City an unknown hand threw in a copy of a Kansas paper containing some sort of an interview with Harvey, who had evidently fallen in with an enterprising reporter, telegraphed on from Boston. The joyful journalese revealed that it was beyond question their boy, and it soothed Mrs. Cheyne for a while. Her one word "hurry" was conveyed by the crews to the engineers at Nickerson, Topeka, and Marceline, where the grades are easy, and they brushed the Continent behind them. Towns and villages were close together now, and a man could feel here that he moved among people.

"I can't see the dial, and my eyes ache so. What are we doing?"

"The very best we can, mamma. There's no sense in getting in before the Limited. We'd only have to wait."

"I don't care. I want to feel we 're moving. Sit down and tell me the miles."

Cheyne sat down and read the dial for her (there were some miles which stand for records to this day), but the seventy-foot car never changed its long steamer-like roll, moving through the heat with the hum of a giant bee. Yet the speed was not enough for Mrs. Cheyne; and the heat, the remorseless August heat, was making her giddy; the clock-hands would not move, and when, oh, when would they be in Chicago?

It is not true that, as they changed engines at Fort Madison, Cheyne passed over to the Amalgamated Brotherhood of Locomotive Engineers an endowment sufficient to enable them to fight him and his fellows on equal terms for ever-more. He paid his obligations to engineers and firemen as he believed they deserved, and only his bank knows what he gave the crews who had sympathized with him. It is on record that the last crew took entire charge of switching operations at Sixteenth Street, because "she" was in a doze at last, and Heaven was to help any one who bumped her.

Now the highly paid specialist who conveys the Lake Shore and Michigan Southern Limited from Chicago to Elkhart is something of an autocrat, and he does not approve of being told how to back up to a car. None the less he handled the "Constance" as if she might have been a load of dynamite, and when the crew rebuked him they did it in whispers and dumb show.

"Pshaw!" said the Atchison, Topeka, and Santa Fé men, discussing life later, "we were n't runnin' for a record. Harvey Cheyne's wife, she was sick back, an' we did n't want to jounce her. Come to think of it, our runnin' time from San Diego to Chicago was 57.54. You can tell that to them

Eastern way-trains. When we 're tryin' for a record, we 'll let you know."

To the Western man (though this would not please either city) Chicago and Boston are cheek by jowl, and some railroads encourage the delusion. The Limited whirled the "Constance" into Buffalo and the arms of the New York Central and Hudson River (illustrious magnates with white whiskers and gold charms on their watch-chains boarded her here to talk a little business to Cheyne), who slid her gracefully into Albany, where the Boston and Albany completed the run from tide-water to tide-water—total time, eighty-seven hours and thirty-five minutes, or three days, fifteen hours and one half. Harvey was waiting for them.

XXIX

THE CHILDREN OF THE ZODIAC

From *Many Inventions*

Though thou love her as thyself,
As a self of purer clay,
Though her parting dim the day,
Stealing grace from all alive,
Heartily know
When half Gods go
The gods arrive.

—EMERSON.

THOUSANDS of years ago, when men were greater than they are to-day, the Children of the Zodiac lived in the world. There were six Children of the Zodiac—the Ram, the Bull, the Lion, the Twins, and the Girl; and they were afraid of the Six Houses which belonged to the Scorpion, the Balance, the Crab, the Fishes, the Goat, and the Waterman. Even when they first stepped down upon the earth and knew that they were immortal Gods, they carried this fear with them; and the fear grew as they became better acquainted with mankind and heard stories of the Six Houses. Men treated the Children as Gods and came to them with prayers and long stories of wrong, while the Children of the Zodiac listened and could not understand.

A mother would fling herself before the feet of the Twins, or the Bull, crying: "My husband was at work in the fields and the Archer shot him and he died; and my son will also be killed by the Archer. Help me!" The Bull would lower his huge head and answer: "What is that to me?" Or the Twins would smile and continue their play, for they could not understand why the water ran out of people's eyes. At other times a man and a woman would come to Leo or the Girl crying: "We two are newly married and we are very happy. Take these flowers." As they threw the flowers they would make mysterious sounds to show that they were happy, and Leo and the Girl wondered even more than the Twins why people shouted "Ha! ha! ha!" for no cause.

This continued for thousands of years by human reckoning, till on a day, Leo met the Girl walking across the hills and saw that she had changed entirely since he had last seen her. The Girl, looking at Leo, saw that he too had changed altogether. Then they decided that it would be well never to separate again, in case even more startling changes should occur when the one was not at hand to help the other. Leo kissed the Girl and all Earth felt that kiss, and the Girl sat down on a hill and the water ran out of her eyes; and this had never happened before in the memory of the Children of the Zodiac.

As they sat together a man and a woman came by, and the man said to the woman:

"What is the use of wasting flowers on those dull Gods. They will never understand, darling."

The Girl jumped up and put her arms around the woman, crying, "I understand. Give me the flowers and I will give you a kiss."

Leo said beneath his breath to the man: "What was the new name that I heard you give to your woman just now?"

The man answered, "Darling, of course."

"Why, of course," said Leo; "and if of course, what does it mean?"

"It means 'very dear,' and you have only to look at your wife to see why."

"I see," said Leo; "you are quite right;" and when the man and the woman had gone on he called the Girl "darling wife"; and the Girl wept again from sheer happiness.

"I think," she said at last, wiping her eyes, "I think that we two have neglected men and women too much. What did you do with the sacrifices they made to you, Leo?"

"I let them burn," said Leo. "I could not eat them. What did you do with the flowers?"

"I let them wither. I could not wear them, I had so many of my own," said the Girl, "and now I am sorry."

"There is nothing to grieve for," said Leo; "we belong to each other."

As they were talking the years of men's life slipped by unnoticed, and presently the man and the woman came back, both white-headed, the man carrying the woman.

"We have come to the end of things," said the man quietly. "This that was my wife——"

"As I am Leo's wife," said the Girl quickly, her eyes staring.

"——was my wife, has been killed by one of your Houses." The man set down his burden, and laughed.

"Which House?" said Leo angrily, for he hated all the Houses equally.

"You are Gods, you should know," said the man. "We have lived together and loved one another, and I have left a good farm for my son: what have I to complain of except that I still live?"

As he was bending over his wife's body there came a whistling through the air, and he started and tried to run away, crying, "It is the arrow of the Archer. Let me live a little longer—only a little longer!" The arrow struck him and he died. Leo looked at the Girl, and she looked at him, and both were puzzled.

"He wished to die," said Leo. "He said that he wished to die, and when Death came he tried to run away. He is a coward."

"No, he is not," said the Girl; "I think I feel what he felt. Leo, we must learn more about this for their sakes."

"For *their* sakes," said Leo, very loudly.

"Because *we* are never going to die," said the Girl and Leo together, still more loudly.

"Now sit you still here, darling wife," said Leo, "while I go to the Houses whom we hate, and learn how to make these men and women live as we do."

"And love as we do?" said the Girl.

"I do not think they need to be taught that," said Leo, and he strode away very angry, with his lion-skin swinging from his shoulder, till he came to the House where the Scorpion lives in the darkness, brandishing his tail over his back.

"Why do you trouble the children of men?" said Leo, with his heart between his teeth.

"Are you so sure that I trouble the children of men alone?" said the Scorpion. "Speak to your brother the Bull, and see what he says."

"I come on behalf of the children of men," said Leo. "I have learned to love as they do, and I wish them to live as I—as we—do."

"Your wish was granted long ago. Speak to the Bull. He is under my special care," said the Scorpion.

Leo dropped back to the earth again, and saw the great star Aldebaran, that is set in the forehead of the Bull, blazing very near to the earth. When he came up to it he saw that his brother, the Bull, yoked to a countryman's plough, was toiling through a wet rice-field with his head bent down, and the sweat streaming from his flanks. The countryman was urging him forward with a goad.

"Gore that insolent to death," cried Leo, "and for the sake of our family honour come out of the mire."

"I cannot," said the Bull, "the Scorpion has told me that some day, of which I cannot be sure, he will sting me where my neck is set on my shoulders, and that I shall die bellowing."

"What has that to do with this disgraceful exhibition?" said Leo, standing on the dyke that bounded the wet field.

"Everything. This man could not plough without my help. He thinks that I am a stray bullock."

"But he is a mud-crusted cottar with matted hair," insisted Leo. "We are not meant for his use."

"You may not be; I am. I cannot tell when the Scorpion may choose to sting me to death—perhaps before I have turned this furrow." The Bull flung his bulk into the yoke, and the plough tore through the wet ground behind him, and the countryman goaded him till his flanks were red.

"Do you like this?" Leo called down the dripping furrows.

"No," said the Bull over his shoulder as he lifted his hind legs from the clinging mud and cleared his nostrils.

Leo left him scornfully and passed to another country, where he found his brother the Ram in the centre of a crowd of country people who were hanging wreaths round his neck and feeding him on freshly plucked green corn.

"This is terrible," said Leo. "Break up that crowd and come away, my brother. Their hands are spoiling your fleece."

"I cannot," said the Ram. "The Archer told me that on some day of which I had no knowledge, he would send a dart through me, and that I should die in very great pain."

"What has that to do with this?" said Leo, but he did not speak as confidently as before.

"Everything in the world," said the Ram. "These people never saw a perfect sheep before. They think that I am a stray, and they will carry me from place to place as a model to all their flocks."

"But they are greasy shepherds, we are not intended to amuse them," said Leo.

"You may not be; I am," said the Ram. "I cannot tell when the Archer may choose to send his arrow at me— perhaps before the people a mile down the road have seen me." The Ram lowered his head that a yokel newly arrived might throw a wreath of wild garlic-leaves over it, and waited patiently while the farmers tugged his fleece.

"Do you like this?" cried Leo over the shoulders of the crowd.

"No," said the Ram, as the dust of the trampling feet made him sneeze, and he snuffed at the fodder piled before him.

Leo turned back, intending to retrace his steps to the Houses, but as he was passing down a street he saw two small children, very dusty, rolling outside a cottage door, and playing with a cat. They were the Twins.

"What are you doing here?" said Leo, indignant.

"Playing," said the Twins calmly.

"Cannot you play on the banks of the Milky Way?" said Leo.

"We did," said they, "till the Fishes swam down and told us that some day they would come for us and not hurt us at all and carry us away. So now we are playing at being babies down here. The people like it."

"Do you like it?" said Leo.

"No," said the Twins, "but there are no cats in the Milky Way," and they pulled the cat's tail thoughtfully. A woman came out of the doorway and stood behind them, and Leo saw in her face a look that he had sometimes seen in the Girl's.

"She thinks that we are foundlings," said the Twins, and they trotted indoors to the evening meal.

Then Leo hurried as swiftly as possible to all the Houses one after another; for he could not understand the new trouble that had come to his brethren. He spoke to the Archer, and the Archer assured him that so far as that House was concerned Leo had nothing to fear. The Water-man, the Fishes, and the Goat, gave the same answer. They knew nothing of Leo, and cared less. They were the Houses, and they were busied in killing men.

At last he came to that very dark House where Cancer the Crab lies so still that you might think he was asleep if you did not see the ceaseless play and winnowing motion of the feathery branches round his mouth. That movement never ceases. It is like the eating of a smothered fire into rotten timber in that it is noiseless and without haste.

Leo stood in front of the Crab, and the half darkness allowed him a glimpse of that vast blue-black back, and the motionless eyes. Now and again he thought that he heard some one sobbing, but the noise was very faint.

"Why do you trouble the children of men?" said Leo. There was no answer, and against his will Leo cried, "Why do you trouble us? What have we done that you should trouble us?"

This time Cancer replied, "What do I know or care? You were born into my House, and at the appointed time I shall come for you."

"When is the appointed time?" said Leo, stepping back from the restless movement of the mouth.

"When the full moon fails to call the full tide," said the Crab, "I shall come for the one. When the other has taken the earth by the shoulders, I shall take that other by the throat."

Leo lifted his hand to the apple of his throat, moistened his lips, and recovering himself, said:

"Must I be afraid for two, then?"

"For two," said the Crab, "and as many more as may come after."

"My brother, the Bull, had a better fate," said Leo, sullenly. "He is alone."

A hand covered his mouth before he could finish the sentence, and he found the Girl in his arms. Womanlike, she had not stayed where Leo had left her, but had hastened off at once to know the worst, and passing all the other Houses, had come straight to Cancer.

"That is foolish," said the Girl whispering. "I have been waiting in the dark for long and long before you came. *Then* I was afraid. But now——" She put her head down on his shoulder and sighed a sigh of contentment.

"I am afraid now," said Leo.

"That is on my account," said the Girl. "I know it is, because I am afraid for your sake. Let us go, husband."

They went out of the darkness together and came back to the Earth, Leo very silent, and the Girl striving to cheer him. "My brother's fate is the better one," Leo would repeat from time to time, and at last he said: "Let us each go our own way and live alone till we die. We were born into the House of Cancer, and he will come for us."

"I know; I know. But where shall I go? And where will you sleep in the evening? But let us try. I will stay here. Do you go on."

Leo took six steps forward very slowly, and three long steps backward very quickly, and the third step set him again at the Girl's side. This time it was she who was begging him to go away and leave her, and he was forced to comfort her all through the night. That night decided them both never to leave each other for an instant, and when they had come to this decision they looked back at the darkness of the House of Cancer high above their heads, and with their arms round each other's necks laughed, "Ha! ha! ha!" exactly as the children of men laughed. And that was the first time in their lives that they had ever laughed.

Next morning they returned to their proper home and saw the flowers and the sacrifices that had been laid before their doors by the villagers of the hills. Leo stamped down the fire with his heel and the Girl flung the flower-wreaths out of sight, shuddering as she did so. When the villagers returned, as of custom, to see what had become of their offerings, they found neither roses nor burned flesh on the altars, but only a man and a woman, with frightened white faces sitting hand in hand on the altar-steps.

"Are you not Virgo?" said a woman to the Girl. "I sent you flowers yesterday."

"Little sister," said the Girl, flushing to her forehead, "do not send any more flowers, for I am only a woman like yourself." The man and the woman went away doubtfully.

"Now, what shall we do?" said Leo.

"We must try to be cheerful, I think," said the Girl. "We

know the very worst that can happen to us, but we do not know the best that love can bring us. We have a great deal to be glad of."

"The certainty of death?" said Leo.

"All the children of men have that certainty also; yet they laughed long before we ever knew how to laugh. We must learn to laugh, Leo. We have laughed once, already."

People who consider themselves Gods, as the Children of the Zodiac did, find it hard to laugh, because the Immortals know nothing worth laughter or tears. Leo rose up with a very heavy heart, and he and the girl together went to and fro among men; their new fear of death behind them. First they laughed at a naked baby attempting to thrust its fat toes into its foolish pink mouth; next they laughed at a kitten chasing her own tail; and then they laughed at a boy trying to steal a kiss from a girl, and getting his ears boxed. Lastly, they laughed because the wind blew in their faces as they ran down a hill-side together, and broke panting and breathless into a knot of villagers at the bottom. The villagers laughed, too, at their flying clothes and wind-reddened faces; and in the evening gave them food and invited them to a dance on the grass, where everybody laughed through the mere joy of being able to dance.

That night Leo jumped up from the Girl's side crying: "Every one of those people we met just now will die——"

"So shall we," said the Girl sleepily. "Lie down again, dear." Leo could not see that her face was wet with tears.

But Leo was up and far across the fields, driven forward by the fear of death for himself and for the Girl, who was dearer to him than himself. Presently he came across the Bull drowsing in the moonlight after a hard day's work, and looking through half-shut eyes at the beautiful straight furrows that he had made.

"Ho!" said the Bull. "So you have been told these things too. Which of the Houses holds your death?"

Leo pointed upward to the dark House of the Crab and groaned. "And he will come for the Girl too," he said.

"Well," said the Bull, "what will you do?"

Leo sat down on the dyke and said that he did not know.

"You cannot pull a plough," said the Bull, with a little touch of contempt. "I can, and that prevents me from thinking of the Scorpion."

Leo was angry, and said nothing till the dawn broke, and the cultivator came to yoke the Bull to his work.

"Sing," said the Bull, as the stiff, muddy ox-bow creaked and strained. "My shoulder is galled. Sing one of the songs that we sang when we thought we were all Gods together."

Leo stepped back into the canebrake, and lifted up his voice in a song of the Children of the Zodiac—the war-whoop of the young Gods who are afraid of nothing. At first he dragged the song along unwillingly, and then the song dragged him, and his voice rolled across the fields, and the Bull stepped to the tune, and the cultivator banged his flanks out of sheer light-heartedness, and the furrows rolled away behind the plough more and more swiftly. Then the Girl came across the fields looking for Leo, and found him sing-ing in the cane. She joined her voice to his, and the culti-vator's wife brought her spinning into the open and listened with all her children round her. When it was time for the nooning, Leo and the Girl had sung themselves both thirsty and hungry, but the cultivator and his wife gave them rye bread and milk, and many thanks; and the Bull found occasion to say:

"You have helped me to do a full half field more than I should have done. But the hardest part of the day is to come, brother."

Leo wished to lie down and brood over the words of the Crab. The Girl went away to talk to the cultivator's wife and baby, and the afternoon ploughing began.

"Help us now," said the Bull. "The tides of the day are running down. My legs are very stiff. Sing, if you never sang before."

"To a mud-spattered villager?" said Leo.

"He is under the same doom as ourselves. Are you a coward?" said the Bull.

Leo flushed, and began again with a sore throat and a bad temper. Little by little he dropped away from the songs of the Children and made up a song as he went along; and this was a thing he could never have done had he not met the Crab face to face. He remembered facts concerning cultivators and bullocks and rice-fields that he had not particularly noticed before the interview, and he strung them all together, growing more interested as he sang, and he told the cultivator much more about himself and his work than the cultivator knew. The Bull grunted approval as he toiled down the furrows for the last time that day, and the song ended, leaving the cultivator with a very good opinion of himself in his aching bones. The Girl came out of the hut where she had been keeping the children quiet, and talking woman-talk to the wife, and they all ate the evening meal together.

"Now yours must be a very pleasant life," said the cultivator; "sitting as you do on a dyke all day and singing just what comes into your head. Have you been at it long, you two—gipsies?"

"Ah!" lowed the Bull from his byre. "That's all the thanks you will ever get from men, brother."

"No. We have only just begun it," said the Girl; "but we are going to keep to it as long as we live. Are we not, Leo?"

"Yes," said he; and they went away hand in hand.

"You can sing beautifully, Leo," said she, as a wife will to her husband.

"What were you doing?" said he.

"I was talking to the mother and the babies," she said. "You would not understand the little things that make us women laugh."

"And—and I am to go on with this—this gipsy work?" said Leo.

"Yes, dear, and I will help you."

There is no written record of the life of Leo and of the Girl, so we cannot tell how Leo took to his new employment which he detested. We are only sure that the Girl loved him when and wherever he sang; even when, after the song was done, she went round with the equivalent of a tambourine and collected the pence for the daily bread. There were times, too, when it was Leo's very hard task to console the Girl for the indignity of horrible praise that people gave him and her—for the silly wagging peacock feathers that they stuck in his cap, and the buttons and pieces of cloth that they sewed on his coat. Woman-like, she could advise and help to the end, but the meanness of the means revolted.

"What does it matter," Leo would say, "so long as the songs make them a little happier?" And they would go down the road and begin again on the old, old refrain—that whatever came or did not come the children of men must not be afraid. It was heavy teaching at first, but in process of years Leo discovered that he could make men laugh and hold them listening to him even when the rain fell. Yet there were people who would sit down and cry softly, though the crowd was yelling with delight, and there were people who maintained that Leo made them do this; and the Girl would talk to them in the pauses of the performance and do her best to comfort them. People would die, too, while Leo was talking and singing and laughing; for the Archer and the Scorpion and the Crab and the other Houses were as busy as ever. Sometimes the crowd broke, and were frightened, and Leo strove to keep them steady by telling them that this was cowardly; and sometimes they mocked at the Houses that were killing them, and Leo explained that this was even more cowardly than running away.

In their wanderings they came across the Bull, or the Ram, or the Twins, but all were too busy to do more than nod to each other across the crowd, and go on with their work. As the years rolled on even that recognition ceased, for the Children of the Zodiac had forgotten that they had ever been Gods working for the sake of men. The star Aldebaran was crusted with caked dirt on the Bull's forehead, the Ram's fleece was dusty and torn, and the Twins were only babies fighting over the cat on the doorstep. It was then that Leo said, "Let us stop singing and making jokes." And it was then that the Girl said, "No." But she did not know why she said "No" so energetically. Leo maintained that it was perversity, till she herself, at the end of a dusty day, made the same suggestion to him, and he said, "Most certainly not!" and they quarrelled miserably between the hedgerows, forgetting the meaning of the stars above them. Other singers and other talkers sprang up in the course of the years, and Leo, forgetting that there could never be too many of these, hated them for dividing the applause of the children of men, which he thought should be all his own. The Girl would grow angry too, and then the songs would be broken, and the jests fall flat for weeks to come, and the children of men would shout: "Go home, you two gipsies. Go home and learn something worth singing!"

After one of these sorrowful, shameful days, the Girl, walking by Leo's side through the fields, saw the full moon coming up over the trees, and she clutched Leo's arm, crying: "The time has come now. Oh, Leo, forgive me!"

"What is it?" said Leo. He was thinking of the other singers.

"My husband!" she answered, and she laid his hand upon her breast, and the breast that he knew so well was hard as stone. Leo groaned, remembering what the Crab had said.

"Surely we were Gods once," he cried.

"Surely we are Gods still," said the Girl. "Do you not remember when you and I went to the House of the Crab and—were not very much afraid? And since then . . . we have forgotten what we were singing for—we sang for the pence, and, oh, we fought for them!—We, who are the Children of the Zodiac!"

"It was my fault," said Leo.

"How can there be any fault of yours that is not mine too?" said the Girl. "My time has come, but you will live longer, and . . ." The look in her eyes said all she could not say.

"Yes, I will remember that we are Gods," said Leo.

It is very hard, even for a child of the Zodiac who has forgotten his Godhead, to see his wife dying slowly, and to know that he cannot help her. The Girl told Leo in those last months of all that she had said and done among the wives and the babies at the back of the roadside performances, and Leo was astonished that he knew so little of her who had been so much to him. When she was dying she told him never to fight for pence or quarrel with the other singers; and, above all, to go on with his singing immediately after she was dead.

Then she died, and after he had buried her he went down

the road to a village that he knew, and the people hoped that he would begin quarrelling with a new singer that had sprung up while he had been away. But Leo called him "my brother." The new singer was newly married—and Leo knew it—and when he had finished singing Leo straightened himself, and sang the "Song of the Girl," which he had made coming down the road. Every man who was married, or hoped to be married, whatever his rank or colour, understood that song—even the bride leaning on the new husband's arm understood it too—and presently when the song ended, and Leo's heart was bursting in him, the men sobbed. "That was a sad tale," they said at last, "now make us laugh." Because Leo had known all the sorrow that a man could know, including the full knowledge of his own fall who had once been a God—he, changing his song quickly, made the people laugh till they could laugh no more. They went away feeling ready for any trouble in reason, and they gave Leo more peacock feathers and pence than he could count. Knowing that pence led to quarrels and that peacock feathers were hateful to the Girl, he put them aside and went away to look for his brothers, to remind them that they too were Gods.

He found the Bull goring the undergrowth in a ditch, for the Scorpion had stung him, and he was dying, not slowly, as the Girl had died, but quickly.

"I know all," the Bull groaned, as Leo came up. "I had forgotten, too, but I remember now. Go and look at the fields I ploughed. The furrows are straight. I forgot that I was a God, but I drew the plough perfectly straight, for all that. And you, brother?"

"I am not at the end of the ploughing," said Leo. "Does Death hurt?"

"No; but dying does," said the Bull, and he died. The

cultivator who then owned him was much annoyed, for
there was a field still unploughed.

It was after this that Leo made the Song of the Bull who
had been a God and forgotten the fact, and he sang it in
such a manner that half the young men in the world conceived that they too might be Gods without knowing it. A
half of that half grew impossibly conceited, and died early.
A half of the remainder strove to be Gods and failed, but the
other half accomplished four times more work than they
would have done under any other delusion.

Later, years later, always wandering up and down, and
making the children of men laugh, he found the Twins
sitting on the bank of a stream waiting for the Fishes to
come and carry them away. They were not in the least
afraid, and they told Leo that the woman of the House had
a real baby of her own, and that when that baby grew old
enough to be mischievous he would find a well-educated cat
waiting to have its tail pulled. Then the Fishes came for
them, but all that the people saw was two children drowning in a brook; and though their foster-mother was very
sorry, she hugged her own real baby to her breast, and was
grateful that it was only the foundlings.

Then Leo made the Song of the Twins who had forgotten
that they were Gods, and had played in the dust to amuse
a foster-mother. That song was sung far and wide among
the women. It caused them to laugh and cry and hug their
babies closer to their hearts all in one breath; and some of
the women who remembered the Girl said: "Surely that is
the voice of Virgo. Only she could know so much about
ourselves."

After those three songs were made, Leo sang them over
and over again, till he was in danger of looking upon them
as so many mere words, and the people who listened grew

tired, and there came back to Leo the old temptation to stop singing once and for all. But he remembered the Girl's dying words and went on.

One of his listeners interrupted him as he was singing. "Leo," said he, "I have heard you telling us not to be afraid for the past forty years. Can you not sing something new now?"

"No," said Leo; "it is the only song that I am allowed to sing. You must not be afraid of the Houses, even when they kill you."

The man turned to go, wearily, but there came a whistling through the air, and the arrow of the Archer was seen skimming low above the earth, pointing to the man's heart. He drew himself up, and stood still waiting till the arrow struck home.

"I die," he said, quietly. "It is well for me, Leo, that you sang for forty years."

"Are you afraid?" said Leo, bending over him.

"I am a man, not a God," said the man. "I should have run away but for your Songs. My work is done, and I die without making a show of my fear."

"I am very well paid," said Leo to himself. "Now that I see what my songs are doing, I will sing better ones."

He went down the road, collected his little knot of listeners, and began the Song of the Girl. In the middle of his singing he felt the cold touch of the Crab's claw on the apple of his throat. He lifted his hand, choked, and stopped for an instant.

"Sing on, Leo," said the crowd. "The old song runs as well as ever it did."

Leo went on steadily till the end, with the cold fear at his heart. When his song was ended, he felt the grip on his throat tighten. He was old, he had lost the Girl, he knew that he was losing more than half his power to sing, he could scarcely walk to the diminishing crowds that waited for him, and could not see their faces when they stood about him. None the less he cried angrily to the Crab:

"Why have you come for me *now?*"

"You were born under my care. How can I help coming for you?" said the Crab, wearily. Every human being whom the Crab killed had asked that same question.

"But I was just beginning to know what my songs were doing," said Leo.

"Perhaps that is why," said the Crab, and the grip tightened.

"You said you would not come till I had taken the world by the shoulders," gasped Leo, falling back.

"I always keep my word. You have done that three times, with three songs. What more do you desire?"

"Let me live to see the world know it," pleaded Leo. "Let me be sure that my songs——"

"Make men brave?" said the Crab. "Even then there would be one man who was afraid. The Girl was braver than you are. Come."

Leo was standing close to the restless, insatiable mouth. "I forgot," said he, simply. "The Girl was braver. But I am a God too, and I am not afraid."

"What is that to me?" said the Crab.

Then Leo's speech was taken from him, and he lay still and dumb, watching Death till he died.

Leo was the last of the Children of the Zodiac. After his death there sprang up a breed of little mean men, whimpering and flinching and howling because the Houses killed them and theirs, who wished to live forever without any pain. They did not increase their lives, but they increased their own torments miserably, and there were no Children of the Zodiac to guide them, and the greater part of Leo's songs were lost.

Only he had carved on the Girl's tombstone the last verse of the Song of the Girl, which stands at the head of this story.

One of the children of men, coming thousands of years later, rubbed away the lichen, read the lines, and applied them to a trouble other than the one Leo meant. Being a man, men believed that he had made the verses himself; but they belong to Leo, the Child of the Zodiac, and teach, as he taught, that what comes or does not come, we must not be afraid.

XXX

THE STORY OF UNG

From *The Seven Seas*

ONCE, on a glittering ice-field, ages and ages ago,
   Ung, a maker of pictures, fashioned an image of snow.
Fashioned the form of a tribesman—gaily he whistled and
   sung,
Working the snow with his fingers. *Read ye the Story of
   Ung!*

Pleased was his tribe with that image—came in their hun-
   dreds to scan—
Handled it, smelt it, and grunted: "Verily, this is a man!
Thus do we carry our lances—thus is a war-belt slung.
Ay, it is even as we are. Glory and honour to Ung!"

Later he pictured an aurochs—later he pictured a bear—
Pictured the sabre-tooth tiger dragging a man to his lair—
Pictured the mountainous mammoth, hairy, abhorrent,
   alone—
Out of the love that he bore them, scribing them clearly on
   bone.

Swift came the tribe to behold them, peering and pushing
and still—
Men of the berg-battered beaches, men of the boulder-
hatched hill,
Hunters and fishers and trappers—presently whispering
low;
"Yea, they are like—and it may be . . . But how does the
Picture-man know?

"Ung—hath he slept with the Aurochs—watched where the
Mastodon roam?
Spoke on the ice with the Bow-head—followed the Sabre-
tooth home?
Nay! these are toys of his fancy! If he have cheated us so,
How is there truth in his image—the man that he fashioned
of snow?"

Wroth was that maker of pictures—hotly he answered the
call:
"Hunters and fishers and trappers, children and fools are
ye all!
Look at the beasts when ye hunt them!" Swift from the
tumult he broke,
Ran to the cave of his father and told him the shame that
they spoke.

And the father of Ung gave answer, that was old and wise
in the craft,
Maker of pictures aforetime, he leaned on his lance and
laughed:
"If they could see as thou seest they would do what thou
hast done,
And each man would make him a picture, and—what would
become of my son?

"There would be no pelts of the reindeer, flung down at thy
 cave for a gift,
Nor dole of the oily timber that strands with the Baltic
 drift;
No store of well-drilled needles, nor ouches of amber pale;
No new-cut tongues of the bison, nor meat of the stranded
 whale.

"*Thou* hast not toiled at the fishing when the sodden tram-
 mels freeze,
Nor worked the war-boats outward, through the rush of the
 rock-staked seas.
Yet they bring thee fish and plunder—full meal and an easy
 bed—
And all for the sake of thy pictures." And Ung held down
 his head.

"*Thou* hast not stood to the aurochs when the red snow reeks
 of the fight;
Men have no time at the houghing to count his curls aright:
And the heart of the hairy mammoth thou sayest they do
 not see,
Yet they save it whole from the beaches and broil the best
 for thee.

"And now do they press to thy pictures, with open mouth
 and eye,
And a little gift in the doorway, and the praise no gift can
 buy:
But—sure they have doubted thy pictures, and that is a
 grievous stain—
Son that can see so clearly, return them their gifts again."

And Ung looked down at his deerskins—their broad shell-
    tasselled bands—
And Ung drew downward his mitten and looked at his
    naked hands;
And he gloved himself and departed, and he heard his father,
    behind:
"Son that can see so clearly, rejoice that thy tribe is blind."

Straight on that glittering ice-field, by the caves of the lost
    Dordogne,
Ung, a maker of pictures, fell to his scribing on bone—
Even to mammoth editions. Gaily he whistled and sung,
Blessing his tribe for their blindness. *Heed ye the Story of
    Ung!*

XXXI

THE SONG OF THE BANJO

From *The Seven Seas*

You could n't pack a Broadwood half a mile—
    You must n't leave a fiddle in the damp—
You could n't raft an organ up the Nile,
    And play it in an Equatorial swamp.
I travel with the cooking-pots and pails—
    I 'm sandwiched 'tween the coffee and the pork—
And when the dusty column checks and tails,
    You should hear me spur the rearguard to a walk!

    With my *"Pilly-willy-winky-winky-popp!"*
        [O it 's any tune that comes into my head!]
    So I keep 'em moving forward till they drop;
        So I play 'em up to water and to bed.

In the silence of the camp before the fight,
    When it 's good to make your will and say your prayer,
You can hear my *strumpty-tumpty* overnight
    Explaining ten to one was always fair.

I 'm the prophet of the Utterly Absurd,
  Of the Patently Impossible and Vain—
And when the Thing that Could n't has occurred,
  Give me time to change my leg and go again.

> With my *"Tumpa-tumpa-tumpa-tum-pa-tump!"*
>   In the desert where the dung-fed camp-smoke curled
> There was never voice before us till I led our lonely
>   chorus,
>   I—the war-drum of the White Man round the
>   world!

By the bitter road the Younger Son must tread,
  Ere he win to hearth and saddle of his own—
'Mid the riot of the shearers at the shed,
  In the silence of the herder's hut alone—
In the twilight, on a bucket upside down,
  Hear me babble what the weakest won't confess—
I am Memory and Torment—I am Town!
  I am all that ever went with evening dress!

> With my *"Tunka-tunka-tunka-tunka-tunk!"*
>   [So the lights—the London lights—grow near and
>   plain!]
> So I rowel 'em afresh toward the Devil and the Flesh,
>   Till I bring my broken rankers home again.

In desire of many marvels over sea,
  Where the new-raised tropic city sweats and roars,
I have sailed with Young Ulysses from the quay
  Till the anchor rumbled down on stranger shores.
He is blooded to the open and the sky,
  He is taken in a snare that shall not fail,
He shall hear me singing strongly, till he die,
  Like the shouting of a backstay in a gale.

With my "*Hya! Heeya! Heeya! Hullah! Haul!*"
    [O the green that thunders aft along the deck!]
Are you sick o' towns and men? You must sign and
        sail again,
    For it 's "Johnny Bowlegs, pack your kit and trek!"

Through the gorge that gives the stars at noon-day clear—
    Up the pass that packs the scud beneath our wheel—
Round the bluff that sinks her thousand fathom sheer—
    Down the valley with our guttering brakes asqueal:
Where the trestle groans and quivers in the snow,
    Where the many-shedded levels loop and twine,
So I lead my reckless children from below
    Till we sing the Song of Roland to the pine.

    With my "*Tinka-tinka-tinka-tinka-tink!*"
        [And the axe has cleared the mountain, croup and
           crest!]
    So we ride the iron stallions down to drink,
        Through the cañons to the waters of the West!

And the tunes that mean so much to you alone—
    Common tunes that make you choke and blow your nose,
Vulgar tunes that bring the laugh that brings the groan—
    I can rip your very heartstrings out with those;
With the feasting, and the folly, and the fun—
    And the lying, and the lusting, and the drink,
And the merry play that drops you, when you 're done,
    To the thoughts that burn like irons if you think.

    With my "*Plunk-lunka-lunka-lunka-lunk!*"
        Here 's a trifle on account of pleasure past,
        Ere the wit that made you win gives you eyes to see
          your sin
        And the heavier repentance at the last.

Let the organ moan her sorrow to the roof—
  I have told the naked stars the grief of man.
Let the trumpets snare the foeman to the proof—
  I have known Defeat, and mocked it as we ran.
My bray ye may not alter nor mistake
  When I stand to jeer the fatted Soul of Things
But the Song of Lost Endeavour that I make,
  Is it hidden in the twanging of the strings?

  With my *"Ta-ra-rara-rara-ra-ra-rrrp!"*
    [Is it naught to you that hear and pass me by?]
  But the word—the word is mine, when the order moves
      the line
    And the lean, locked ranks go roaring down to die.

The grandam of my grandam was the Lyre—
  [O the blue below the little fisher-huts!]
That the Stealer stooping beachward filled with fire,
  Till she bore my iron head and ringing guts!
By the wisdom of the centuries I speak—
  To the tune of yestermorn I set the truth—
I, the joy of life unquestioned—I, the Greek—
  I, the everlasting Wonder Song of Youth!

  With my *"Tinka-tinka-tinka-tinka-tink!"*
    [What d'ye lack, my noble masters? What d'ye
      lack?]
  So I draw the world together link by link:
    Yea, from Delos up to Limerick and back!

XXXII

"THE LINER SHE'S A LADY"

From *The Seven Seas*

THE Liner she's a lady, an' she never looks nor 'eeds—
The Man-o'-War's 'er 'usband, an' 'e gives 'er all she
    needs;
But, oh, the little cargo-boats, that sail the wet seas roun',
They're just the same as you an' me a-plyin' up an' down!

    Plyin' up and down, Jenny, 'angin' round the Yard,
    All the way by Fratton tram down to Portsmouth 'Ard;
    Anythin' for business, an' we're growin' old—
    Plyin' up an' down, Jenny, waitin' in the cold!

The Liner she's a lady by the paint upon 'er face,
An' if she meets an accident they call it sore disgrace:
The Man-o'-War's 'er 'usband, and 'e's always 'andy by,
But, oh, the little cargo-boats! they've got to load or die.

The Liner she's a lady, and 'er route is cut an' dried;
The Man-o'-War's 'er 'usband, an' 'e always keeps beside;

But, oh, the little cargo-boats that 'ave n't any man!
They 've got to do their business first, and make the most
they can.

The Liner she 's a lady, and if a war should come,
The Man-o'-War 's 'er 'usband, and 'e 'd bid 'er stay at home;
But, oh, the little cargo-boats that fill with every tide!
'E 'd 'ave to up an' fight for them, for they are England's
pride.

The Liner she 's a lady, but if she was n't made,
There still would be the cargo-boats for 'ome an' foreign
trade.
The Man-o'-War 's 'er 'usband, but if we was n't 'ere,
'E would n't have to fight at all for 'ome an' friends so dear.

'Ome an' friends so dear, Jenny, 'angin' round the Yard,
All the way by Fratton tram down to Portsmouth 'Ard;
Anythin' for business, an' we 're growin' old—
'Ome an' friends so dear, Jenny, waitin' in the cold!

XXXIII

THE KING

From The Seven Seas

"FAREWELL, Romance!" the Cave-men said;
  "With bone well carved he went away;
Flint arms the ignoble arrowhead,
  And jasper tips the spear to-day.
Changed are the Gods of Hunt and Dance,
And he with these. Farewell, Romance!"

"Farewell, Romance!" the Lake-folk sighed;
  "We lift the weight of flatling years;
The caverns of the mountain side
  Hold him who scorns our hutted piers.
Lost hills whereby we dare not dwell,
Guard ye his rest. Romance, farewell!"

"Farewell, Romance!" the Soldier spoke;
  "By sleight of sword we may not win,
But scuffle 'mid uncleanly smoke
  Of arquebus and culverin.
Honour is lost, and none may tell
Who paid good blows. Romance, farewell!"

241

"Farewell, Romance!" the Traders cried;
  "Our keels ha' lain with every sea;
The dull-returning wind and tide
  Heave up the wharf where we would be;
The known and noted breezes swell
Our trudging sail. Romance, farewell!"

"Good-bye, Romance!" the Skipper said;
  "He vanished with the coal we burn;
Our dial marks full steam ahead.
  Our speed is timed to half a turn.
Sure as the tidal trains we ply
'Twixt port and port. Romance, good-bye!"

"Romance!" the Season-tickets mourn,
  "*He* never ran to catch his train,
But passed with coach and guard and horn—
  And left the local—late again!
Confound Romance!" . . . And all unseen
Romance brought up the nine-fifteen.

His hand was on the lever laid,
  His oil-can soothed the worrying cranks,
His whistle waked the snow-bound grade,
  His fog-horn cut the reeking Banks;
In dock and deep and mine and mill
The Boy-god reckless laboured still.

Robed, crowned and throned, he wove his spell,
  Where heart-blood beat or hearth-smoke curled
With unconsidered miracle,
  Hedged in a backward-gazing world:
Then taught his chosen bard to say:
"The King was with us—yesterday!"

XXXIV

RECESSIONAL

From *The Seven Seas*

GOD of our fathers, known of old—
    Lord of our far-flung battle-line—
Beneath whose awful Hand we hold
    Dominion over palm and pine—
Lord God of Hosts, be with us yet,
Lest we forget—lest we forget!

The tumult and the shouting dies—
    The captains and the kings depart—
Still stands Thine ancient Sacrifice,
    An humble and a contrite heart.
Lord God of Hosts, be with us yet,
Lest we forget—lest we forget!

Far-called our navies melt away—
    On dune and headland sinks the fire—
Lo, all our pomp of yesterday
    Is one with Nineveh and Tyre!
Judge of the Nations, spare us yet,
Lest we forget—lest we forget!

If, drunk with sight of power, we loose
    Wild tongues that have not Thee in awe—
Such boasting as the Gentiles use,
    Or lesser breeds without the Law—
Lord God of Hosts, be with us yet,
Lest we forget—lest we forget!

For heathen heart that puts her trust
    In reeking tube and iron shard—
All valiant dust that builds on dust,
    And guarding calls not Thee to guard—
For frantic boast and foolish word,
Thy mercy on Thy People, Lord! Amen.

XXXV

L'ENVOI

From *The Seven Seas*

W<small>HEN</small> Earth's last picture is painted, and the tubes are
    twisted and dried,
When the oldest colours have faded, and the youngest critic
    has died,
We shall rest, and, faith, we shall need it—lie down for an
    æon or two,
Till the Master of All Good Workmen shall set us to work
    anew!

And those who were good shall be happy: they shall sit in
    a golden chair;
They shall splash at a ten-league canvas with brushes of
    comet's hair;
They shall find real saints to draw from—Magdalene, Peter,
    and Paul;
They shall work for an age at a sitting and never be tired
    at all!

And only the Master shall praise us, and only the Master
shall blame;
And no one shall work for money, and no one shall work for
fame;
But each for the joy of the working, and each, in his separate
star,
Shall draw the Thing as he sees It for the God of Things
as They Are!